P9-DUU-073

DEATH IN THE QUADRANGLE

DEATH IN THE QUADRANGLE

by

EILÍS DILLON

WALKER AND COMPANY
New York

First published in Great Britain in 1956. First published in the United States of America in 1968 by Walker and Company, a division of the Walker Publishing Company, Inc.

Library of Congress Catalog Card Number: 68-31211.

Printed in the United States of America from type set in Great Britain.

1

Living in rather too comfortable retirement at Crane's Court, Professor Daly was overjoyed at the invitation to give the Keyes Lectures at his old college. The Keyes Lectures consisted of an annual series of ten lectures, given by an eminent literary man, on the vast subject of the Novel. The fee offered was large enough to command respect, though not so large as popular rumour declared it to be. Professor Daly cared little for this, for he had an adequate income of his own. What really pleased him was the honour which the invitation conferred upon him.

Though he was the author of a vast number of books, no one would have called Professor Daly an eminent literary man. His purple novels were written under the pseudonym of Rosemary Downes, and had fluttered the hearts of dowagers and scullery-maids alike over a great many years.

"But at last someone has awoken to the fact that five of my students have become really good writers," he said to himself with satisfaction.

If he had had an audience he would have wiped away an imaginary tear as he finished:

"It's my misfortune that I taught like an angel and wrote like poor Poll."

And with a fluttering heart he posted a cool reply accepting the invitation.

Some weeks later, with ten well-composed lectures in his dispatch-case, he took the train for Dublin. He knew that his lectures would be good, and that he could give himself up with a free mind to the enjoyment of this brief return to his old way of life.

Since his retirement four years ago, Professor Daly had rarely visited the King's University of Dublin, where he had been

7

Professor of English Language and Literature for over thirty years. He had deliberately weaned himself away from the academic life, so as to spare himself some of the nostalgic pain of retirement. He had been successful in a great measure. Crane's Court was as near to perfection as a hotel can be. The murder of the late owner and Daly's close association with the solution of the mystery, had given him a pleasantly possessive feeling towards the hotel and its new owners. He liked the good-humoured informality of Galway, the astonishing beauty of its environs and the ready acceptance there of himself as a great man.

But as the train rattled its way through Dublin to the station, he found himself quoting uneasily:

"He who is a great man in a small town would do well to stay there."

Still, he reflected that it might be good for his rather stout ego to be made to feel small for a few weeks, for though he expected to be sufficiently honoured within the College, he could not hope that the traffic would stop and stare every time he passed through O'Connell Street.

It was a joy to breathe the smutty air of Dublin again. He took a taxi to the Phoenix Park, as if he intended to visit the zoo, and then walked slowly along to the tall arched gates of the College.

The King's University of Dublin, founded by George III, consisted of only one College. Its situation was the happiest possible, adjoining the Phoenix Park. Beyond the gateway with its porter's lodge, the ground rose a little, so that the main buildings stood on a small eminence. They formed three sides of a square, the fourth side being open to the sun. From the quadrangle thus formed the avenue sloped away down towards the main gates. The original buildings were of old red brick, warm with age, and strangely at peace with the others of later dates that were scattered here and there throughout the College Park. The open parts of the park were planted with single oaks and elms, so that the expanses of grass between were pleasantly broken up. At the foot of the hill, over to the left, a good-sized river flowed gently down to join the Liffey. It was known to the

8

students as the Styx, and was used for rowing practice in the proper season, to the understandable annoyance of the swans that owned it.

King's College was largely residential, the rooms being all contained in the main building. There were two-roomed suites for students, as was the custom in the golden days when the College was built. There were slightly larger suites for unmarried members of the staff. The President's Lodging occupied the right wing of the quadrangle. Thus the students were fortunate in being able to observe academic life at very close quarters indeed, and they never failed to appreciate this privilege.

Walking up the avenue to the main building, Professor Daly found that he might almost have been seeing it all for the first time. It was late October and the Michaelmas Term had begun a fortnight ago. The trees were in their autumn beauty, and their solitary stillness smote his heart. The old red buildings glowed peacefully in the afternoon sun. He went into the main hall and stood hesitating, feeling an almost intolerable loneliness. This was an alien and a frightening sensation for him. He was rescued from it by a middle-aged porter who darted out of a little office at the back of the hall and scurried towards him.

"Good evening, Professor! Well, it's like old times to see you walking in through that door again. And how are you at all? And how are they all below in Galway?"

He was shaking Daly's hand and pawing his shoulder while he talked, as so many people feel entitled to do to the old. Though he had always disliked this man for his cunning, insinuating ways, Daly was grateful to him now for the warmth of his welcome. He disengaged himself deftly and said:

"Good evening, Jennings. It's good to be back."

He had no intention of replying to the slightly derisive question about the health of the people of Galway. He went on quickly:

"There is room for me in College, I believe?"

"In your old rooms, sir," said Jennings eagerly. "They're vacant at the moment, and the President said we were to put you in there."

9

He seized Daly's suitcase and led the way up the wide, polished staircase, chattering irritatingly all the while.

"You'll see great changes here, sir, since your time. Great changes. The President is a great man. Oh, a great man!"

"A very able man," said Daly gently, pained at the smallness of Jennings's supply of adjectives.

" 'Twould take yourself to think of the word, sir," said Jennings, looking at him with delight. "An able man, indeed."

Patronizing little So-and-so, thought Daly, glancing sideways at Jennings. A moment later he reproached himself for his harshness. It was no wonder that Jennings had developed a patronizing manner, after a quarter-century of playing nursemaid to professors. He hurried to make a friendly remark:

"I don't know the President very well. I was acquainted with him years ago, before he was appointed Professor of Mineralogy, but he had only been in College a year when I retired."

"That's right, sir," said Jennings. " 'Twas a pity he couldn't carry on with the mineralogy after he became President. But sure he couldn't be everywhere."

"Professor Gleeson succeeded him, I think?" said Daly.

"That's right, sir. A quiet sort of a man. The students say he's not a patch on Professor Bradley."

"Students always say that," said Daly tolerantly. "I remember Professor Gleeson as a very clever man indeed. Students like to be talking about the good old times. The greatest numskull is labelled a genius once he has retired."

"That's right, sir, of course," said Jennings coolly. "Sure they say the same about Professor Badger, sir, that he's only trotting after yourself."

They had reached the outer door of Daly's old rooms, and Jennings's face was blank while he opened the door and led the way in. He appeared to be all unconscious of the implications of his last remark, though this seemed hardly possible. Daly found himself quite uncomfortable until Jennings had placed his suitcase in the bedroom and had left him alone. Then he went over to the tall, embrasured windows of the study, and stood for a long time looking down on the drowsy quadrangle. Except for a brief interval once, and for occasional holidays, he had lived in these rooms for thirty years. He knew every tree and shrub in the park as well as he knew his own face in his shaving glass. Even the students who rambled about in groups seemed exactly the same, as if their lives had been suspended in time like the lovers on a Grecian urn. He saw one or two of his ageless former colleagues, still lost, no doubt, in thoughts of academic viciousness.

The room behind him was painfully familiar too, so that he could hardly bear to turn around at last and examine it. Then he saw that it had not changed at all either. The panelled walls, the wide oak fireplace, the deep, commodious bookshelves now empty, were the same as they had always been. The leather-covered armchairs and the leather-topped library table were the same that he had always used. Even the long, brass fire-irons were set at their familiar angle. He thought it rather cruel of Bradley to have put him in these rooms again. But Bradley was a thick-skinned fellow, and he might have imagined that he was doing him a kindness.

He was roused at last by a double tap on the door, and a moment later a querulous-looking old man in a green apron trotted into the room.

"Lewis!" said Daly. "I'm going to weep on your shoulder!"

Lewis allowed himself a momentary smile before he resumed his habitual expression of pain and disillusion.

"Glad to see you, sir," he said, in the tones of a man who has drunk life to the lees and found it sour. "Jennings should have told me you were coming this afternoon. I'd have lit the fire. I'd have dusted the rooms. I'd have——"

"Never mind, Lewis," said Daly soothingly. "It's not Jennings's fault. I didn't tell anyone the exact hour at which I expected to arrive."

"You should have sent a telegram," said Lewis reproachfully. "People can't be expected to be inspired about the time you're going to come. I'd have had your tea ready——"

He stopped suddenly, as if he had realized the futility of trying to teach a retired professor how to behave. Then he said waveringly:

"Seeing you standing there made me think it was old times, sir. But the old times were never like this."

Lewis had always looked as sad as an old mother turned out into the snow on Christmas Eve. The difference now was that he no longer seemed to revel in his sorrows.

"Jennings tells me that Professor Bradley is a fine President," Daly said innocently.

"Jennings would say that," said Lewis bitterly. "Jennings is the boy that will mind what he says, even to yourself, sir, and make sure to curry favour in high places. Jennings is a person of No Principle." He shook his head slowly. "There's terrible changes here, sir, enough to make the old President, God be good to him, turn in his grave."

Daly doubted the truth of this, remembering how hard it had been to induce the late President to turn in his chair, even while he was alive. Bradley's administration would be entirely different. The late President, who had been Professor Blake of Archaeology, had reigned throughout Daly's association with King's College. He had had a mania for jigsaw and crossword puzzles, and had believed that his health profited by spending fourteen hours out of the twenty-four in bed. Somehow his work had got done, and the College had had a cheerful, lotus-eating air about it during his time. In the absence of tension, also, research work had progressed at a great rate, so that on the whole it was hard to call Blake a failure.

"Blake was King Log," Daly thought, "and if I'm not very much mistaken, Bradley has turned out to be King Stork. He was the type for drastic changes and no nonsense."

And he felt a little glow of relief that he had been safely retired before the accession of this new dynasty.

He told Lewis that he had had tea, and eased him gently out of the room. It was clear that Lewis wanted to pour out the accumulated grievances of several years, but Daly felt that it would be unkind to encourage him. The fortunate Jennings had seen that his best plan was to become an admirer of Bradley. It was a pity that this had been impossible for Lewis.

After the old man had gone out, a little huffily, Daly found

12

himself surprisingly free from his former nostalgia. He wagged a metaphorical finger at himself and said:

"You are a wicked old fellow, to be so quickly consoled at the trials of others."

But it was with an irrepressibly cheerful grin that he went downstairs and out into the quadrangle in search of some members of the staff who would tell him more of their common misfortunes.

He had no sooner reached the front steps, however, than Jennings came hurrying towards him from the direction of the President's Lodging. It was too late to fly.

"The President knows you're here, sir," Jennings panted. "He wants to see you at once. I'll take you over."

"By no means! I'd like to see if I can remember the way," said Daly.

He left Jennings looking slightly disconcerted, and started off across the quadrangle to the President's front door. On the way he encountered a stooped, long-haired little man, who looked twenty years older than Daly but was in fact five years younger. They stopped and the little man shook Daly's hand heartily and painfully. When he could trust his voice not to shake, Daly said:

"It's good to see you, Delaney. I thought you had retired."

"One more year to go," said Delaney. "Only one more year. I have a very important job in hand, that I must get finished with before I go. Yes, very important. I hope I'll have time for it; though it's more a question of opportunity than time."

"What is it?" asked Daly, who was finding this rather difficult to follow.

"I'll tell you some day soon," said Delaney, earnestly fixing large trusting eyes, under shaggy white eyebrows, on Daly's face. "We heard you were coming. I've been looking forward to telling you. Where are you going now?"

"To see Bradley." Daly nodded in the direction of the President's Lodging. "He's waiting for me."

"Bradley turned out to be a rat, did you know?" said Delaney mildly.

13

"Lewis has been telling me that things have changed since he took over," said Daly.

Delaney sighed.

"I find his energy depressing," he said. "You'll see."

He waved vaguely and moved on, an oddly shaped little figure, bulging mysteriously in unexpected places. Feeling a little uneasy now, Daly continued on his way, and found his heart pounding ridiculously while he waited for the door to be opened to his knock.

His fears of personal embarrassment were soon stilled. Bradley greeted him with hearty affection in his study, and settled him down with a glass of sherry in front of a blazing wood fire. Watching him from the depths of an armchair, Daly noticed that Bradley had aged a little. He looked his full sixty years now, though he was as bouncy as ever. He had developed the slightly watchful air of all Presidents. His strong, black hair had a heavier sprinkling of grey, and his waistcoat had taken an outward curve. Since he was tall and broad-shouldered, the effect was dignified. Bradley had always been a handsome fellow, and his new air of authority and assurance became him well. The only trouble, thought Daly, is that professors hate to be treated with authority and assurance.

"Why do you never come to see us?" Bradley was saying. "There is always room for you. You shouldn't cut yourself off from us."

Daly felt a little glow of pleasure, and his critical attitude to Bradley softened. Though he could not actually like him, there was no denying that Bradley cut a far better figure than old Blake, whose somnolent, heavy body, coated in cigarette ash, had been an offence in itself. In Blake's time, this room had been a shambles, littered with old newspapers and small tables with partly finished jigsaw puzzles. Daly remembered one—a map of the world, with vast expanses of blue sea in hundreds of tiny pieces of nightmare similarity. The very recollection of it made him experience again the terrible feeling of frustration, like a man lost in a maze, which had possessed him when first he had caught sight of it. But Blake had finished it, down to the last triumphant, futile piece, and had invited

14

his friends in then, like the woman in the Gospels, to rejoice with him.

"Who cleaned up this place when Blake died?" he asked curiously.

"Miss Blake did that," said Bradley, looking a little surprised. "She set two chimneys on fire, burning the crosswords. Old Delaney got into a great state of excitement. He wanted to divert the smoke under the floors to smoke out the rats."

"Is he still talking about rats?" asked Daly.

As he spoke he remembered that Delaney had mentioned rats even in their brief conversation.

"Yes, he still has rats on the brain," said Bradley. "I only hope he'll get to the end of his time without causing trouble."

"Do you think he has got worse?" Daly asked anxiously. "I met him just now and he seemed the same as usual."

"He talks about rats on the Academic Council now," said Bradley. "He never used to do that. I saw some of the younger men laughing at him the other day. One could hardly blame them, really. He made quite a scene. We were talking about this new money that we have been offered, and Delaney thumped the table and shouted that this college would be no good until we had got rid of the rats. I really blushed for the poor old man. It was dreadful."

"Did he get any support?"

"Oh, Milligan saved his face for him very nicely. He said he quite agreed with him, and that he thought we should enter in the minutes our recommendation that before any money is spent on the buildings, we should banish the rats. Delaney was pleased at that, and he spent the rest of the time nodding solemnly to himself, looking the picture of a man who has made his point. The meeting finished soon after, though. We all felt a sudden need for fresh air."

"Milligan is a good fellow," said Daly. "That was a kind thing to do."

"He made himself unpopular by it, though," said Bradley. "I don't mind telling you that several members of the staff have been in to ask me to retire Delaney at once. They would have been glad if we had had to have him hauled off by the Guards."

"Can they not wait one year, until he is seventy?" said Daly. "He's a first-rate archaeologist."

"That is why there is no valid excuse for pushing him out," said Bradley. "Miss O'Leary is leading the anti-Delaney party, because she is terrified of rats. Every time she sees Delaney, she thinks of them."

Miss O'Leary had been one of Daly's most brilliant students. She had abandoned English literature for Irish, and was now Professor of Celtic languages. Like most professors, Daly was prejudiced against all subjects except his own, and he had always thought Irish a somewhat unlikely enthusiasm for a lively young woman of thirty. She was one of the most beautiful women that he had ever seen, quite tall and very slender, with jet-black hair and searching dark blue eyes. In her dealings with her fellow-man she was a ravening wolf, but Daly knew it was true that she was terrified of rats. A great many of her colleagues were equally terrified of her, for she was a relentless enemy. She had a magnificent command of language, which she used to curl up an opponent or to support an ally as the occasion demanded. Daly thought that if she started a movement to have Delaney retired, it would take all of Bradley's reserves of power to oppose her successfully. But it was doubtful if Bradley wanted to oppose her. It was clear enough that he was only too anxious to remove Delaney. Daly sighed for his poor old friend, whose chances of finishing his last year at the College seemed slim indeed.

He dragged his thoughts away from the fascinating convolutions of university politics to hear Bradley say:

"When do you give your first lecture?"

"On Thursday at noon, I believe. That gives me a day to look over my papers."

"Ah, yes," said Bradley indulgently. "You may have quite a large audience. The students have been working up an amount of publicity. They tell me that quite a number of outsiders have put their names down for the series."

It was the custom of the College to invite the public to the Keyes Lectures. In order to prevent overcrowding, however, people who wished to come were asked to register their names

16

with the College. This usually had the effect of making them attend at every lecture, no matter how dull the speaker, almost as if they had paid for the privilege. It also kept casual sight-seers and frivolous people away. The effect of an earnest bloc on the students was mercifully dampening. Apart from this consideration, Daly, like most professors, delighted in lecturing to the general public. He tried to cover his gratification, but Bradley was sharp enough to see it and crude enough to comment on it.

"I thought you would be pleased," he said. "The outsiders keep the students quiet."

"I have never found my students inattentive," said Daly gently.

"Of course not," said Bradley heartily. There was a pause, which Daly occupied by drinking his sherry. Then Bradley said, in a different, confidential tone: "Were you surprised at being invited to give the lectures?"

Daly raised his eyebrows.

"I should not be surprised if I were offered the Nobel Prize," he said blandly.

But he felt a prickle of irritation. Bradley was a tactless fool, without a doubt. Now he was laughing heartily.

"Witty as ever!" he crowed, while Daly watched him coldly. "The Nobel Prize! Well, well!"

"Think of that!" said Daly softly.

"Still you must have been surprised," Bradley was saying. "I arranged it myself, you see."

Daly sat up straight and asked sharply:

"Why have the students worked up outside publicity?"

"Oh, that is just to annoy Badger. You need not take any notice of Badger."

"I could murder this man," Daly said to himself as he sat back carefully in his armchair. Aloud he asked:

"Why did you have me invited to give the Keyes Lectures, Mr. President?"

Like the echo of an avalanche, hollow-sounding and shaken, came the answer:

"Because I believe that someone is planning to murder me."

2

The secret of Professor Daly's good humour was that he could never remember his personal grievances. They commanded his attention for a moment only, until they were replaced by something more interesting. He sat up now to stare at Bradley. The suddenness of his movement sent a minute splash of sherry on to his coat sleeve. He got out his handkerchief and blotted it absently while he observed the change that had come over the President.

Bradley was clearly making a determined effort to retain an appearance of detached amusement. But his smile flashed on and off like a defective electric bulb, and his eyelids twitched with fear. He jerked a little in his chair. His hands grasped each other for comfort and fell apart again unconsoled. When he spoke his voice was husky, until he gave a little nervous cough.

"I'm sure you think I'm a fool, Daly. But I know I'm right. I thought of you at once."

"But it's a couple of months since I was invited to give the lectures," Daly pointed out.

"I knew I was safe during the long vacation," said Bradley. "Not enough people about."

"Why do you think you are going to be murdered?" Daly asked. "Perhaps you take your position too seriously. All Presidents' lives are threatened, sooner or later."

"Do you think so?" said Bradley eagerly. He brightened for a moment and then said bitterly: "I didn't think you would laugh at me."

"I'm not laughing at you," Daly protested. "It's quite true. All big public figures get anonymous letters threatening their lives."

"How did you know about the anonymous letters?" Bradley asked sharply.

"I didn't," said Daly. "But they are part of the pattern. Have you got them here? I should like to see them. They are often very revealing."

"I'm afraid I have burnt them," said Bradley.

But his eye had travelled quickly across to the Nelson rent table that stood between the windows.

Daly gave no sign that he had noticed, but he wondered if the letters were locked into one of the drawers.

"What did they say?" he asked.

"Oh, a lot of nonsense," said Bradley. He laughed without humour. "But I have no doubt that there was a threat to my life. There were all sorts of wild accusations about my so-called persecution of the staff, and a strong suggestion that I am planning to pinch the Leahy money."

"What is the Leahy money?" Daly asked patiently.

"Leahy is an odd little duck, an Irish-American industrialist. He has a stack of money that he wants to give to the College. We are trying to work out a scheme that will please him and still be useful to us. You remember, I was telling you just now that Delaney wants to spend it on exterminating the rats."

"Have you got any rats, by the way?" Daly asked curiously. "There were none in my time."

"Not that I know of," said Bradley, "unless you count Delaney himself."

Daly studied the President for a moment before he said:

"Then it is some time since you began to get the letters."

"Three months and more," said Bradley. "I get one every Tuesday by the second post."

"Have you had one to-day?"

"Yes," said Bradley curtly.

"In what way is your life threatened?"

"They are all the same," said Bradley, making a renewed effort to appear detached. "First comes a list of my so-called crimes. Then at the foot of the page there is a picture of a little tombstone, in ink, with my name on it. It's quite nerve racking, I can assure you."

19

"I have no doubt of that," said Daly. "And clearly a threat of some kind. Have you not thought of telling the police?"

"Of course not," said Bradley shortly. "That is quite impossible. There would be publicity, and heavy-handed enquiries. It would all be most unsuitable."

Daly tried to fix his face into a sympathetic expression while he considered the whole story. An honest man who believed that his life was threatened would have called in the Guards at once. He began to wonder why Bradley had been so hesitant. His eyes certainly had that blank appearance of a man who does not feel comfortable in the company of the police. To be sure, Daly had seen the same look on people with tender consciences, whose lives were made miserable if they forgot to water the geraniums or feed the cat. But he happened to know that Bradley's conscience was not especially tender.

"Why did you think that I could help you?" he asked at last.

"I read your evidence at the Crane's Court trial," said Bradley. "It was patent that you had observed a great deal more than most people. I know no one else that I can trust. And you understand university life. Please do not let me down."

"Of course I'll help you," said Daly, "but I can't do it alone. I have no authority to question people."

"You have my authority," said Bradley tartly.

Daly did not point out that this was not worth a fig. Again he noticed perspiration on Bradley's forehead, in spite of his attempt to appear merely angry. It was a great many years since anyone had threatened to murder Daly, but he still respected the effect that such a threat can produce.

"Besides," continued Bradley, "it is essential that no one knows you are asking questions for a purpose. It must look like mere curiosity. I don't want people to know that I commissioned you to look after me. And that reminds me, I'm not asking you to do this for nothing. You can name your own fee. I'll spare no expense."

Daly found these continual embarrassing turns in the conversation very trying. He managed to shelve the question of a fee for his services without actually stating that he was not a professional detective, and hurried on to the next point:

"If I find out who is writing the letters, I take it that you will have no objection to calling in the Guards then?"

"If you find out who is writing the letters," said Bradley emphatically, "I'll deal with him in my own way. The Guards must not be brought into the business at all."

"I should not attempt to deal with it," said Daly judicially. "If you face the person in question with his guilt, he may murder you in real earnest."

He said this deliberately and brutally, for he was convinced of its truth. Bradley waved the idea aside and said:

"Don't you worry. I'll be able for him, once I know who he is. Your only business is to discover that, and leave the rest to me."

Daly had his own ideas about this, but it was clear that there was no further point in discussing them. Bradley was saying bitterly:

"You won't find it hard to get the staff talking about me. Just let them think you disapprove of me, and you'll find yourself surrounded with people bursting to discourse on my sins. I never courted popularity. I never pandered to them, nor flattered them as they would have liked. But I got the work done, all right, which is more than can be said for most presidents."

And he sat back and stroked his stomach, waiting for Daly to agree that this policy had been sound. Daly had long ago ceased to wonder that anyone had threatened to murder Bradley. The surprising thing was that he had been left so long alive. Possibly what had saved him was the fact that professors are not usually practical people. Even if they worked out a dozen methods of murdering Bradley, unless they could hand on the actual task to a research student, nothing would ever be done.

Daly stood up to go, saying:

"I'll ask questions here and there, and see if I can find out who is behind all this. But if I do find out, I won't tell you his name until after we have again discussed the question of calling in the Guards."

21

"Very well," said Bradley, with a contemptuous shrug for such scruples. "Just find out, as you say, and we'll talk about the other question afterwards."

It was clear that he had no doubt of his power to persuade Daly to part with the information when the time would come.

"And perhaps he will, in spite of me," thought Daly, as he walked back to his rooms across the quadrangle.

Lewis had got the fire going in his study, and had pulled the leather-topped table into exactly the position that Daly had always favoured. His dispatch-case lay on the table, and Lewis would have ferreted through it to see if the lectures were any good, if Daly had not taken the precaution of locking it. He opened it now, took out a bundle of papers and tried to settle down to read. He had to give it up after a short time. Usually his own words fascinated him, so that he would read on and on as if he were in a dream. But this evening he lost interest after half a page, and his mind kept returning to Bradley's plight. At last he put down the papers and gave himself up to consideration of it, and of his own connection with it.

It was not only by chance that Professor Daly had been associated with the solution of several murder mysteries. The psychology of murderers had always had a terrible attraction for him. In his younger days he had made a game of spotting potential murderers—selfish, vain, short-sighted, often stupid people who seemed capable of becoming obsessed with hatred, so that the only solution of their difficulties appeared to be in the death of their enemy. He had become so expert at his game that he had more than once spotted murder when no one else had suspected it. Then he had kept his own counsel and watched while the murderer, though never accused of his crime, was eventually and inevitably destroyed by his own conscience. On the rare occasions when he had joined in the pursuit, he was far too sensitive and intelligent not to have suffered agonizing qualms afterwards. For this reason he had recently resolved firmly to turn his back upon all murderers and their tantrums.

But Bradley's case was surely different, he pleaded with himself. Perhaps this was an opportunity such as he had never been offered before, actually to save a man from being murdered. This time he would not have to watch helplessly, since he had been asked to interfere. It would be cruel and heartless to refuse.

"There you go again," he said to himself severely. "I knew you would not be able to resist."

He felt his hands go clammy in sympathy as he remembered Bradley's fear.

It was characteristic of him that he wasted no time in speculating about his next move. The room had grown dark, except for the dancing flames of the fire which were reflected in dull pools of light on the panelling. He heaved himself out of his chair and went across to close the heavy tapestry curtains. At all sides, lighted windows shone out on to the dark quadrangle, making the grass look more velvety and brilliant than it could ever have done in the daytime. The red-curtained windows of the President's Lodging had a solid, comfortable air. Daly wondered what Mrs. Bradley thought of all this. It seemed either that Bradley had not told her of his fears for his life, or else that she had failed to comfort him. It was possible that Bradley had not wished to worry her pretty head, but Daly thought it far more likely that Mrs. Bradley was kept for her usefulness only, and that Bradley never discussed his affairs with her at all.

He went downstairs to the public telephone in the hall, and a moment later he was inviting his friend, Inspector Mike Kenny of the Civic Guards, to dinner at the College.

"In the plainest of plain clothes, Mike, if you please. Take the shoulder pads out of your coat. Wear pointy-toed shoes. Red socks, if possible. A *white* shirt. And a decent silk tie. No, not a flamboyant one—frightful word, that! And no darting of the eyes about, taking notes on the cuff, measuring of the floor, asking to see licences, or any of that sort of thing. I'm not sure what your profession is to be, but I shall have thought of something by the time you come."

He hung up with a sigh, released the handle of the booth door, which he had been clutching to make sure that no one could hear, and went off to the restaurant to book a table for himself and for his guest.

It was typical of King's College that no one had thought of inviting Professor Daly to dinner on his first evening in the College. He had not expected it. He knew that his former colleagues would all notice him sitting in the dining-room, would look at their watches and suddenly realize what date it was, and then come scurrying, rambling or trotting over to make their apologies and fight among themselves about who should have him first. But for this evening he was free, and Inspector Kenny would have an invaluable chance of observing the antics of professors against their native background.

Some time later, he waited for Mike in the main hall, and looked him over judicially before admitting that he would do.

"The suit is a trifle loud, perhaps," he said, "but I think we may turn that to account."

"It's Connemara tweed," said Mike hotly, "and anyway it's the best one I have."

"I was wondering if it wasn't too good," Daly explained gently. "Wait until you see how the others are dressed. You must not take me for a typical professor."

He smoothed his beautiful waistcoat with pride.

An aged man hurried past, dressed in greenish evening clothes of a very old-fashioned cut. Mike looked after him in alarm.

"You said nothing about evening clothes——"

"No, no," Daly soothed him. "That was Professor Milligan. He is the only one who wears evening clothes. He says he won't get any more when that suit is worn out."

As they went towards the dining-room, Mike asked:

"Are things done very formally? I have never had a meal here before."

"Just like an ordinary restaurant," said Daly, "except that the food is very good. At one time there was a high table, and port, and much better food for the staff than for the students, grace in Latin and I don't know what. But all that has changed. Now the professors feel most thankful to the students for letting them eat in the same room with them at all. I like it better this way, I must say. The other thing used to frighten the visitors."

24

Though he dared not let Professor Daly see it, Mike was very much impressed with his first sight of the College dining-room. The panelled walls and high windows invested it with an exciting strangeness. The polished parquet floor reflected light from four splendid Waterford glass chandeliers. There were round tables with white linen cloths, and table-napkins as big as winding-sheets. Professor Milligan was seated at his table, unfolding his napkin, as they came in.

"English educational Gothic, this part of the building," said Daly, "but it impresses people, for some reason. The chandeliers are magnificent."

Above the heavy oak door an inscription was carved, not very expertly. Daly grasped Mike's sleeve and pointed to it with pride.

"This was carved by a student called Murphy, in the year of the great famine," he said. "I mean the great College famine, of course, in 1830, when the food was so bad that the fat students trembled for their skins and the thin ones died like flies. It's an ancient Irish proverb, composed by Murphy himself, I believe: 'Ní léanta go líonta.' That is, as I need hardly interpret to a Galway man, learning cannot thrive on an empty stomach. It has been left there ever since as a warning to the powers that order the food."

They sat at a table at one end of the long room.

"You are a school inspector, I think, with that suit," said Daly, leaning back to observe Mike impartially. "Galway graduate—Master's degree, of course. Subjects, Irish, history. Some taste for mathematics, but one has to make a choice. Western district—Mayo would be best. You have come to Dublin to hand in your reports. You could post them, of course, but you enjoy the little trip, and you like meeting your friends in the department."

"What is my salary, please?" Mike asked meekly.

"It doesn't arise. Gentlemen never discuss such things. It must be lower than a professor's, of course. Better not to think of it at all, if you can."

"I'll try not to."

It was half-past seven and the room was rapidly filling up.

Daly had placed Mike well, so that he had an uninterrupted view down the length of the room. There were no women present.

"We keep them in a corral at the other end of the building," Daly explained in answer to Mike's question. "They don't have dinner, of course. That would be far too good for them. They just have luncheon, and in the evening they fend for themselves as best they can. Tea, I believe, in cafés in the town."

"Do they live in the College?"

"Good Lord, no! What an idea! They were only let in on sufferance about fifty years ago, and we are watching them ever since for signs of insubordination."

Mike noticed that the tables by the walls were occupied by the staff, while the students took the middle of the room. He asked if there was any reason for this.

"Purely instinctive," said Daly. "Very few professors would feel easy if the students were behind them. It's an elementary precaution. After all, as they would tell you, if Agamemnon had locked the bathroom door, he would be alive to-day."

Mike was silenced for some minutes by this statement. They had artichoke soup, thick with cream, served at great speed by a long, lean waiter, who ran down the room with a line of plates on his arm, distributing them one by one with a strange little bow every time. Mike was fascinated.

"Forty years, man and boy, I suppose?" he said.

"Only thirty," said Daly. "They age young. I don't know what we do to them."

They had cutlets, curled up and clothed in batter. In a low voice, Daly began to tell him who the different people were, with little details about each which made it easy for Mike to append characters to them.

"We have coffee in another room," said the old man, as soon as the cheese had come. "You'll meet them then. The President always comes over."

And now at last he told Mike why he had asked him to dinner. Deliberately, Mike had not hurried him, for Daly always had a way of building up his background before coming to the main business. Mike knew that time was not being

26

wasted, and that it was more profitable to concentrate on the information that he was being offered than to speculate impatiently about the reason why he had been summoned at all.

"So you see why you must meet all the people who are connected with Bradley," said Daly.

"And Bradley himself, of course," said Mike.

"In a way, Bradley is the least odd of them all. But that only makes it harder to understand him."

As Daly had foreseen, before they left the dining-room a procession of his former colleagues marched upon him. They had waited until they had finished dinner, and Professor Kelly, in his fear that Daly would escape, had left his table in such a hurry that he was holding a half-eaten cheese biscuit in his hand. As soon as they found that he was going to take coffee with them, they relaxed a little, and the whole party moved out of the dining-room. The door of the adjoining room stood open. Presently Mike was standing before a blazing fire, holding his coffee cup and being introduced to one after another of Daly's friends. They looked him over sharply and were extremely affable.

"They like you for being so tall and thin and ascetic-looking," said Daly in his ear. "Such a contrast with their own waistlines."

"They are all much too fat," said Professor Fox emphatically.

He was a tall, heavy-faced man of about fifty. Daly had said that he was a zoologist. Mike remembered this because of his appropriate name.

"Have you a good diet just now?" Daly asked mischievously, in the tone that one might use to ask if he had a good cook.

"Excellent," said Fox. "You just eat nothing at all."

"How extraordinary," murmured Daly. "You remind me of the story of the Ballyvourneyman's donkey."

"What was that?" asked Fox suspiciously.

"Just when he had taught it to live without food", said Daly, "didn't it go and die on him."

"Very funny," said Fox coldly. "I was speaking figuratively, of course." Daly, who hated imprecision above all things, raised his eyebrows at this. "What I mean is that I eat the minimum at meals, and have a little snack between them, so that I won't get too hungry. I planned to lose two stone in six weeks, but I'm afraid it's not working as well as I thought it would."

"That's because you eat sweets all the time," said a young man who was standing by. "Why don't you just eat everything and see what happens? I believe in being happy."

"Obviously," said Fox nastily, with a meaning eye on the young man's waistcoat.

He seemed not to mind in the least, and smiled at Fox's back as the older man stumped away.

"This is Professor Hamilton," said Daly to Mike. "He's just back from America. How does it feel to be a professor, Hamilton?"

"No more getting up at half-past six," chanted Hamilton. "Running up a ladder with a hod full of bricks. No more tobacco—nothing but cigars. For I am the driver on the new tramcars!"

Daly beamed at him delightedly.

"I do like a man who can count his blessings," he said.

Hamilton winked at Mike. He was very short, with a round head which would soon be bald. He had the comfortable, calculating eye of a baby. His coffee was heaped with cream.

Professor Delaney came across, holding his saucer at a slant so that Mike waited in agony for the cup to slide to the floor. Strolling after him, smirking, came a thin elderly man with an unpleasant face. He took no notice of Mike, beyond a distant nod, and addressed himself to Daly.

"Have you heard about Delaney's latest idea?" he drawled. "Do tell them, Delaney."

"I meant to, Burren," said Delaney eagerly. "That's what I came over for." He turned his back to them, lifted his coat-tails and said: "Feel!"

"I beg your pardon?" said Daly, looking disconcerted for the first time in Mike's experience.

"No need," said Delaney briskly. "Go on, feel!"

Daly put out an unwilling hand and felt, while Burren took a sip of his coffee with an expression of derision which Mike found almost insupportable. Daly withdrew his hand after one poke and said uneasily:

"What is it, Delaney?"

"Dunlopillo," said Delaney triumphantly. "I have a sort of pocket built into the lining of my trousers, and the little cushion just slips in. It took my tailor a long time to understand what I wanted, but he does now. I'll give you his name, if you want to get it done—it only costs five shillings for the pocket. The cushion is more, of course, but you can use the same cushion for all your trousers." He pirouetted. "And you would hardly notice it. The comfort is unbelievable. I wish I had thought of it years ago. You really must try it, Daly."

Mike chuckled aloud at the vision of Daly's suave contours distorted with a cushion. Delaney turned eagerly to him.

"Wonderful idea, isn't it? You could hardly believe the difference it makes. I can sit down anywhere now, in the greatest comfort. It's marvellous for a long sermon, or a public lecture, or for sitting on a wall when I'm making notes during a dig. I don't know why it has never been thought of before."

"I can't imagine," Burren sneered. "Have you thought of taking out a patent?" .

"What a splendid idea, Burren!" Delaney's cup wobbled while he seized Burren's hand and shook it. "What a clever fellow you are to have thought of it! I must see about it first thing in the morning. Oh, dear! I hope my tailor has not got there first. He's quite capable of it—a most unscrupulous man. I caught him showing it to another customer."

While Delaney chattered on, Mike became aware that silence had fallen upon the other groups of men standing about the room. It was a watchful, uneasy silence. All their eyes were turned towards the door. Delaney, suddenly unhappy, stopped and looked into the fire, as if he had no interest in the man who had appeared in the doorway. Glancing quickly at the faces around him, Mike felt the little needles of their hatred run through him.

"Bradley," said Daly's voice in his ear.

3

Daly's face wore an eager little smile quite inappropriate to the atmosphere of the room. It was clear that he had not known how universal nor how strong was the hatred of Bradley. Mike found himself holding his breath like a man under water, so that it was quite painful when he released it.

At first glance it was not obvious why Bradley should be so disliked. He looked solid and dependable, Mike thought, the sort of man who would take the burdens of departmental administration off the unwilling shoulders of the professors. But he looked as if he might take everything else off them, too. He gave his assembled colleagues one glance of amusement, and made straight for Daly.

"I didn't know we had a guest," he said reproachfully. "I should have come in much sooner."

A spontaneous burst of chatter began. Delaney slipped away to a far corner and hid behind Professor Fox who immediately turned around and offered him his bag of sweets. Out of the tail of his eye Mike saw him take one with an expression of gratitude. Now Daly was introducing him to Bradley, with a tissue of lies for his history. Bradley held his hand for longer than is usual and gazed at him with large, deep, insincere eyes. Daly watched them for a moment and then moved away through the room. Mike and Bradley were left as it were on an island by the fire. Bradley seemed quite unconcerned, but Mike wished that Daly had stayed a little longer, if only to increase their number to three.

The President chatted pleasantly about the College and its history. Then he began to ask questions about Mike's so-called work. Only that he knew Daly would not have put him into such a false position without very good reason, Mike would have been furiously angry. Any moment now it seemed, he must say something foolish and be exposed for a fraud. But after a moment he observed that Bradley was not really listening to his answers. He seemed only to recall his mind for long enough to ask another intelligent-sounding question in sequence with the last. Then his eyes were darting around the room again, dwelling for an instant on one face after another, as if he were looking for something which he was not certain of recognizing.

"He is looking for his enemy," thought Mike.

"He is looking for a friend," thought Daly, and smiled at Bradley's unresponsive face from a far corner of the room.

Professor Fox, to whom Daly was talking, had been about to offer him a sweet out of his little bag. Now he changed his mind, took one himself, held it under his nose for a moment before putting it into his mouth, and returned the bag to his pocket. Daly was rather relieved, for he was careful about not putting on weight. Fox went on with telling him about the sins of Bradley.

"Fellow belongs to no church," he was saying querulously. "That's very awkward in Ireland. Never know where you are with him. Makes him too independent."

"But he's a good administrator?" Daly said.

"Too good. Little boys watching to see you're in time for lectures. Your income stated in every detail to the Income Tax sharks. A damn' nuisance, in fact."

"Things couldn't have gone on as they were under Blake," Daly pointed out.

"Bradley is a crook," said Fox, bringing the word out carefully, pronouncing it to rhyme with shook, as if he had learned it from a ten-year-old nephew. "You have only to look at him."

They were joined by Milligan, who said:

"Not talking about Bradley, are you? His name should be taboo. He brings out the worst in all of us."

"Perhaps it's just as well," said a gloomy voice behind him. "Better let it out than bottle it up. We're a sad lot. We don't deserve any better of the world——"

"Badger, how are you?" Daly was shaking hands delightedly with the newcomer. "Glum as ever, I see."

A shadowy smile wrinkled Badger's face, his dark blue eyes flashed and sparkled for a second, and went cold again. He was in his early forties, of medium height with nondescript, mouse-coloured hair, rather thin, and a parchment complexion which gave him an unreal appearance, like a bad stained-glass window. His eyes were his most striking feature, for he could not altogether veil their remarkable intelligence. He had the turned-down mouth of a neurotic. The tone of his voice, which was meant to be Socratic and detached, had a distinctly querulous note. Daly entered into lively discussion with him. Fox began to offer Milligan a sweet, changed his mind and put the bag in his pocket without taking one himself either.

"A happy family," Bradley was saying. "A university should be like a happy family. Don't you agree?"

"Yes," said Mike doubtfully.

In the happiest family that he knew, the various members rarely met except for meals. Suddenly he was seized with a desire to tell the truth.

"I don't think that a large group is ever like a happy family," he said. "It's a fine achievement to get them to look happy even for a little while every day."

Bradley glanced at him sharply and said:

"I am rather tired to-night. One should never express platitudes. I'm always doing it. Yes, it has a civilizing influence, this meeting for coffee every evening. Will you come to dinner to-morrow evening at my house? I'm asking Daly."

"I'm not staying in the College, you know," Mike pointed out gently.

"I know," said Bradley. "But if you wouldn't mind coming again to-morrow—I have a number of people coming—I should like to know you better——"

"I'll come, then," said Mike. "It's very kind of you."

But Bradley was not listening. His eyes were roaming around the room again, while he seemed to be trying to catch the drops of conversation that sprayed as far as where he was standing. Mike felt a sudden sharp pang of pity for him.

Though he had never met him before, he could see that Bradley's self-confidence must have been his stock-in-trade. Without it he was a hollow man indeed. Mike met frightened men every day in the course of his business. He longed to declare himself to Bradley and offer his help, but he knew that this would not do. Bradley was not a child. He probably despised himself for feeling frightened, and would react by spurning Mike's offer and denouncing him as a mountebank. This was not to be risked at any cost.

The group was breaking up now and Daly was weaving his way across the room towards them. Bradley had suddenly begun to talk feverishly to Mike about the importance of vocational schools, the poor man's university, the countryman's best preparation for the battle of life, the backbone of the country. It did not require much perspicacity to see that he was only talking so that he would not have to greet his colleagues in any way as they passed by. When he became aware that Professor Daly was at his elbow he dried up as abruptly as he had begun.

Daly gave no sign that he had heard a word. Bradley made great play of disposing of his cigarette-end in the fire, while Mike and Daly waited. By the time he had dropped it twice in the hearth, and had at last managed to throw it into the fire, the room was empty of all but themselves. Then Bradley seemed to grow again to his normal size. He seized Daly and Mike by an elbow each, all unconscious that he was giving great offence to both by doing so, and steered them out of the room, talking very fast.

"Mr. Kenny is having dinner with us to-morrow night, Daly," he said. "You'll both be a great help in entertaining Leahy for me. I've been putting off having Leahy because I needed some outsiders to talk to him. He's not at all the academic type, ha-ha. At seven o'clock, if you please, and quite informal. Good night. So glad to have met you, Kenny."

Mike and Professor Daly stood on the steps and watched him march off across the quadrangle towards his own house.

"Not at all the academic type," Daly quoted meditatively. "So you and I will not feel small with Leahy, Mike."

33

"Oh, I don't think he means it like that," said Mike. "At least not for you."

"He thinks I'm a funny old man, academically," said Daly. "That does not please me. Still, I'm flattered at being asked for my help within my little limits."

"I'm surprised at your being so bitter," said Mike mildly.

"There's something about him that arouses inimical feelings in everyone," said Daly. "I wonder what it is. I suppose it's his self-absorption, really. He can't conceal his opinion that we are unimportant and naturally we don't like that."

"It depends on whether you are accustomed to thinking yourself important," said Mike mischievously.

Before Daly could reply, Professor Badger came down the stairs and crossed the hall to join them.

"I don't know why we put up with this coffee business," he said at once. "It's most frightful tyranny. No one enjoys it. We're a lot of sheep, really, to let him do it to us."

"It's down in the Charter," said Daly. "Fellows taking such meals together, or something. You'll admit it's better than dining at a high table."

"I should have to resign if we went back to that," said Badger. "You're going to Bradley's dinner to-morrow night, I hear?"

"I was not invited," said Daly, "but I gathered that I am expected. Mike, here, is coming, too. Special invitation in his case, to talk about the weather to Leahy."

Badger shot an uninterested look at Mike and grunted. Then he said:

"Well, I have some work to do. See you later, Daly, when you're free."

With another quick hostile look at Mike he walked off.

"Really, Professor Daly! Your friends!" said Mike.

"Not my fault," said Daly complacently. "I do what I can with them, but you can't make a silk purse out of a sow's ear." He stepped out into the quadrangle. "Come for a walk down to the river. It's bright enough, with that moon."

They were silent as they passed through the quadrangle and until they came to a wide gravelled path that went downhill

34

towards the river. The moonlight silvered the stones. It was very quiet. A little breeze blew the sound of the traffic away from them. The city might have been a hundred miles away, if the night sky had not been red with neon lights.

"Badger is not a bad fellow," said Daly after a while. "He was one of my first students. The trouble with him is that English Literature turned and bit him. All those gloomy chaps that you and I would avoid, Badger laps up. He loves the Russians, and those modern fellows who are so preoccupied with sin. The result you see. The years like great black oxen tread the world, and poor old Badger is broken by their passing feet. At his back he always hears Time's winged chariot hurrying near. Under the bludgeonings of chance his head is bludgy but unbowed. You know the kind of thing. Rather rough on the students, when they are just at the suicidal age anyway. I used to try to keep them cheerful. Badger prefers to mar the merriment as you and I fare on our long fool's errand to the grave."

"Is he capable of murder?" Mike asked.

"Always the little policeman," said Daly. "It's hard to say, I doubt if a man who talks about death as much as Badger does would be realistic enough to commit murder. Death is just a beautiful idea to him at the back of it all. Badger laid out, surrounded by lilies, Mrs. Badger and the little Badgers in floods of tears, sympathy on all sides, great man passes away. But no fun if he couldn't open one eye and see it all for himself."

" 'And I'll hear ye all cry over me: Oh, why did you die?' " Mike quoted, having caught the habit from the old man. Daly chuckled and said:

"That's it."

Presently he asked:

"What did you think of them all? Do you think Bradley should take the threats in the anonymous letters seriously?"

"Everyone should take threats seriously," said Mike. "He'll have to show the letters, of course. It's difficult to do anything without them, but if we once got our hands on them, it should not take long to find out who is writing them."

"Is it so easy?"

35

"Quite easy, I assure you."

"Then I'll try again to persuade him to let me have them to-morrow," said Daly. "But I doubt if I'll have any success."

They had reached the river now. The moon laid a path across it, as if they could have walked to the other side. They stood and watched the flickering water slide past. Then Mike said:

"One could not conclude anything from that gathering to-night. They are certainly under some strain, every one of them. But that could be because they don't like the custom of having coffee together——"

"It could be, indeed," said Daly. "I always enjoyed it, but then I am more gregarious than most of them. The average professor likes to creep away to his burrow after a meal and contemplate the infinite. Still, I never remember that little ceremony being so painful."

"You saw what happened when the President came in," said Mike.

"Oh, he's quite right to be frightened," said Daly seriously. "I hardly believed him until they all went silent. Do you think I should advise him to go away?"

"That would be quite the best thing that he could do," said Mike firmly. "He should hand over the letters to the Guards and give us a chance of getting to the bottom of it all. He would be much safer out of the way while the investigations are going on."

"I doubt very much if he will agree to that," said Daly. "He was very insistent that the Guards were not to be brought in. And I feel that I have treated you badly, too, Mike. I was so sure that you would dismiss the whole affair as academic oddity. Now I see that you could not possibly have done that." He sighed deeply. "I'm getting old and tired. I find I can't bear to feel that we can do nothing to save Bradley."

As they turned to walk back to the College he leaned on Mike's arm, as if he had suddenly become too weak to make the ascent alone.

It was not until they had reached the quadrangle that he broke the silence.

36

"I'll have a talk with Badger about Bradley. He may be able to help. I can't take him into my confidence, of course, but I'll lead the conversation around until we get talking about Bradley. Badger has a very penetrating mind."

"I hope he hasn't penetrated my thin disguise," said Mike.

They arranged to meet the next evening and go to Bradley's dinner-party together. Then Professor Daly waved to Mike and bounded up the front steps two at a time. Mike grinned to himself in the darkness at the difference between the vigorous reality and Daly's picture of himself as a tired old man. The promise of a glorious gossip with Badger had put an anticipatory light in his eye which he could not conceal.

Mike's professional interest was thoroughly aroused now. He would have given a great deal to have been allowed to listen to that conversation. He consoled himself with the assurance that he would hear it all from Professor Daly in due course.

On the next evening Mike reached the College at half-past six. Lewis brought him upstairs to Daly's rooms. The old man looked up from his papers and began to gather them together as he said:

"Good evening, Mike. Bradley spotted you last night."

Mike had just shut the door. He leaned against it suddenly and looked at Daly in horror.

"That's right," said the old man, apparently unperturbed. "He's a sharp fellow, as I told you. He remembered seeing a photograph of you in the papers, and he knew I had some friends among the Guards. Don't take it so hard."

Mike tried to sound casual as he asked:

"What was his reaction?"

"He was rather pleased, you know. I certainly felt a fool when he told me, and I think he liked that, too. He would never have called in the Guards himself, but I think he feels much safer now that they are taking an interest in him."

"I certainly can't have dinner with him to-night," Mike began, but Daly interrupted:

"Of course you must. He said so particularly. He said he had spotted you before he asked you to come, and he asked me to tell you so. I think it was rather nice of him to have told

37

me before the dinner party. I should have felt much worse if he had waited until afterwards."

"Well, then, is he prepared to talk to me about the threats to his life?"

"No. You can only communicate with him through me. He says policemen make him uneasy."

"And can I see the anonymous letters?"

"Out of the question. He still says he burned them. Later on, if he gets more frightened, he may show them. But not now."

Feeling very much relieved that there was still almost half an hour to go before he must meet Bradley, Mike sat down and tried to put his confused thoughts in order. If he had not been dealing with a university president, he would have sworn that Bradley had a murk in his past. Else why should policemen make him uneasy? Law-abiding people rather like policemen as they would like and admire a good dog. Mike guessed from his experience, as Professor Daly had done, that the accusations in the letters could contain at least some proportion of truth. He could imagine many ways in which Bradley could have faltered from the path of virtue. That face with its hooded eyes was the face of a highwayman.

"At first I was quite put out," Daly was saying, "but then I began to see that this clears the air. It means you can come to the College again——"

"But what is the use of that if Bradley won't talk to me?" Mike asked angrily. "What am I supposed to do?"

"You are to observe the staff and students and see if any of them look like murder."

"The staff all looked like murder last night," said Mike. "Bradley saw that for himself. And you know I'm not a free-lance detective. I doubt if any such thing exists in Ireland, since we are so grossly under-produced in the matter of crime. I'll have to put myself right with my bosses. I'm going to look very silly, if I don't watch out."

"I should say you have done nothing to be ashamed of so far," said Daly judicially. "If you were patrolling your beat in the city——"

"I don't patrol a beat," said Mike indignantly.

38

"All the better, for my parallel," said Daly complacently. "If you were proceeding home after your day's work and saw someone acting suspicious-like, you would stalk, discover and apprehend him to the best of your ability. Even a private citizen would be expected to do that. How much more so a guardian of the law, whose conscience never sleeps? In this College you have been persuaded that something queer is happening. The Guards have not been called in, there is no tangible reason why you should stand at the front gate and blow your little whistle. But you feel that it would be well to keep an eye on the situation from within, since the opportunity has been offered you. Isn't this true?"

"Yes," said Mike reluctantly. "If I slunk off now, and then if something—went really wrong, I should feel that I had neglected my duty——"

"Exactly!" said Daly triumphantly. "Then conscience would gnaw at your duodenum and afflict it with ulcers. We must not risk that."

"But I'll have to explain the whole thing to my superior officer in the morning," said Mike. "I can't just walk off in the daytime without saying where I am going."

"Can't you?" Daly was disappointed. "Well, I suppose you can't. Is he a reasonable sort of a chap?"

"Very reasonable. I rather think you will see too much of me in the next few days. You may take it that the police won't like it if anything happens to Bradley."

"Neither will Bradley," said Daly dryly.

"Did you learn anything from Professor Badger last night?"

"I refreshed my memory about Bradley's history," said Daly. "It was not very easy to get Badger to talk about him. One would almost think he had made a vow not to mention his name. We had a talk about the Keyes Lectures first, and about the English department, and how the standard of manners among students has declined. I don't remember Badger being exceptionally mannerly when he was a student, but he seems to think the modern student is worse. I told him this was a sign of age in him. I said——"

"How did you get him talking about the President?" asked

39

Mike, fearing that Daly was about to embark on his favourite game of repeating his own witticisms.

Daly looked at him reproachfully.

"I'm coming to that. I took Bradley's own advice. I said that the President was developing a politician's paunch, that I was glad I did not have to live with him, that he looked as if he enjoyed wielding power, and so on. I dropped these remarks one by one, and at last he rose. I played him for a few minutes, and then I certainly got what I wanted. I think I told you about old Blake, who was born old Blake, and did crosswords and jigsaws and died in the odour of dust and tobacco ash?"

"Yes, I have often heard you discourse on Blake," said Mike.

"Well, it seems that Freedom shrieked when Bradley got the job," said Daly. "He sees that all the rules are kept. He makes them all toe the line. They come in time for their lectures, hand in their examination papers on the appointed day, ask permission if they want to be away for a few days, notify him if they get married or die, keep off the grass, don't park their bicycles against the hedges, send in reports and rolls at regular intervals——"

"Sounds just like ordinary life to me," said Mike in amusement.

"It's hell to them," said Daly simply. "They are all hypersensitive, and they can't bear pin-pricks. Large injustices they would almost enjoy. But these daily shacklings of their former glorious freedom are bitterly resented. And it all comes to a head with the arrival of Leahy."

"The same Leahy who is coming to dinner to-night?"

"Yes. It's not every day of the week that a fat little Irish-American comes along with an offer of money for the College. Professors rather pride themselves on being able to manage the finances of their Colleges. Bradley has them on a sore point there, though he is so thick that he may not know it. He has patted them on the head and advised them to keep to the things that they understand and leave Leahy and his money to him. Each of them wants a whack of that money—not for himself, of course, but for his department. They don't trust the President to handle the business properly."

"But have they a right to be consulted?" asked Mike, who knew very little about how such affairs are managed in universities.

"In theory they must be consulted," said Daly, "but a president has very wide powers, and he can, if he likes, present them with a *fait accompli* from which it will be difficult to change. Besides, there is Leahy himself, who admires the President, and will agree to almost anything that will please him."

"What I cannot understand", said Mike at last, "is how Bradley came to be made President at all."

"He was a snake-charmer," said Daly. He waved an elegant hand. "You know how these things happen. He was a graduate of this College who went off to Africa and became quite celebrated as a consulting mineralogist. We were always hearing traveller's tales about how clever and successful he was, and what glory he reflected on his College. He made a stack of money there, too, and presently in his later middle age he took ship and set sail for the land of the Gael where his heart had always been. The professorship of mineralogy became vacant and Bradley applied for it—just for old time's sake, he said. Of course he won hands down. We were always showing him off to visitors as the great man who by a stroke of fortune was humble enough to spend his declining years with us."

"Was he a successful professor?"

"Young man," said Daly severely, "there is no such thing as an unsuccessful professor. Anyway, he wasn't one for long. Within two years of his appointment old Blake died. I had just retired. Bradley laughingly allowed his name to be put forward, and here he is."

"Why did they appoint him?" Mike asked curiously. "Surely they must have known by then what he was like."

"Professors are simple souls at bottom," said Daly. "They liked the idea of Bradley more than they liked Bradley himself. He was new and fresh to most of them. His reputation in his subject was prodigious—deservedly so, I think. And above all,

41

he was wealthy. They felt that a man who does not need anxiously to watch the price of eggs would give more distinction to the business of being the President. There is some justice in that assumption, though there is that little snag about the camel going through the eye of a needle. Of course I have this by hearsay only. I rather lost touch after I retired, for one reason and another."

"Tell me about Bradley's household," said Mike. "Who will be there to-night? Is there a wife and family?"

"A wife, but no family," said Daly after a short pause. "I knew Mrs. Bradley—rather well, at one time. I haven't seen her since I came, but no doubt she will be there to-night."

"How did you know her? Did she not live in South Africa with her husband?"

"Oh, yes, for most of the time. But she is a Dublin woman. It's all so long ago." He paused again, and then went on: "I remember Bradley's testimonials that he brought from South Africa. He had been connected with one or two universities there. They said his presence always stimulated the intellectual life wherever he went. I thought there was a distinct note of menace in that statement. He certainly has stimulated the intellectual life to a fury since he came here." He stood up. "Come along now, young Mike. It's time we went over and enjoyed his hospitality."

Mike looked up in despair from the depths of his armchair.

"How can you seem so unconcerned? I'm quite certain to fall over the carpet, and break my glass, and spill my soup——"

"Nonsense, man! Where's your self-control? Don't you dare let me down!"

"All right, all right." Mike heaved himself to his feet. "It's a strange fact that I never feel embarrassed for my profession until I am in your company."

The old man chose to accept this as a compliment. He swung the door open with a complacent flourish, and they started off for the President's Lodging.

4

On Bradley's doorstep Mike experienced an almost uncontrollable longing to run away. His wide-open eyes and his long, thin face gave him something of the appearance of an anxious snail, as Professor Daly unkindly told him.

"Look happy, honoured, hungry if you like," he said, "but for heaven's sake don't look apologetic. Now you are worse than ever," he wailed as Mike wilted before his eyes.

Fortunately the door was opened just then by Jennings, who acted as Bradley's butler on these occasions. Professor Daly replaced his air of elegant dignity as if it had been a hat, and led the way into the hall. Mike followed him in a fog of unhappiness, through which he quite failed to observe his surroundings. Jennings removed his overcoat for him and bore it away. Dimly he saw Bradley advancing through an open door in front of him.

Then suddenly the air cleared. Bradley was shaking his hand, welcoming him, leading him in, introducing him to the other guests as if he were especially proud of him. He gave no sign whatever of his knowledge of Mike's real profession. He even forbore from naming his fictitious occupation, as he might have done if he had wished privately to enjoy Mike's embarrassment. Mike was very grateful to him for this.

Bradley's drawing-room was a long, fine room with three tall windows looking into a private garden. They were curtained now against the night, in red brocade. The Sheraton furniture, the Waterford glass and Sèvres china, and the Persian rugs all betokened a household where there had never been any children. Their museum-like perfection was faintly depressing, in spite of the comfort of the armchairs and sofas.

Mrs. Bradley, to whom he was introduced first, was rather a

surprise to Mike. She was so small that her head was strained backwards to look up at him, like a child's. Her figure was generously curved, but well controlled, probably at great expense. Her hair was a respectable grey, perfectly waved and with a faint blue rinse. Her expression was friendly and cheerful, except when she glanced at her husband. Then she looked anxious and unhappy. She greeted Mike warmly and then turned to Professor Daly with a nervous giggle.

"I'm so glad to see you," she said. "Why don't you ever come when you are in town?"

To Mike's astonishment a little flush crept over Daly's face. He took her hand for a moment and said:

"You are looking well, Helen. It is nice to see you."

She laughed skittishly. Her husband called her sharply then and she had to turn away to greet another guest. Mike found himself standing with Professor Daly a little apart from the rest, drinking a cocktail with a lot of vermouth in it.

"Nasty stuff, isn't it?" said Daly, lifting his glass and eyeing the contents appreciatively. "I always did hate vermouth."

"I had no idea that you were so closely acquainted with our hostess," said Mike in a low voice.

"Mrs. Bradley and I are old friends. I'm sure I told you that," said Daly. He looked across the room at her, where she stood giggling and smiling at a short stout man who could be no one but Mr. Leahy. "Amazing woman, isn't she? Awfully well preserved for fifty-eight. She possesses the secret of eternal youth, which consists in wearing one's false teeth at night."

Mike was watching Mr. Leahy and wondering for the thousandth time how it was that Americans of his type were as easily recognizable as if they had been Chinese.

Mr. Leahy was short and yellow and his waistline had the uncompromising outward curve of a rubber ball. His hair and moustache and eyebrows were long and white and bristling. The set of his mouth showed plainly what his accent would be. His age might have been anything from sixty to seventy-five. His large, round, grey eyes were very sharp and he had a strange trick of lowering one eyebrow and opening the other eye very wide, as if this helped him to understand the motives of the person with whom he was conversing. Mike would have liked to talk to him, for he always found self-made men fascinating. He warned himself that he was not at Bradley's party for pleasure, however, and began to ask Daly about the other people present.

"There's Badger," said the old man. "And that is Mrs. Badger two steps behind him. She knows her place, poor lady. Tatty, isn't she? You'd never think she has a Master's degree in chemistry, would you?"

Mike thanked heaven that the room was so large that Daly's remarks could not be overheard. Really, he thought, the old man was becoming quite outrageous. But what a strangely clear little picture he could give of a personality in a few words. Mrs. Badger wore an unbecoming grass-green crêpe dress with a cheap lace collar. The scaffolding of her underwear showed clearly through the clinging material. The hemline was uneven. Her hair was a faded blonde, in a kind of bird's nest of tangles. Her complexion was mottled, and she used no artifice to conceal it. But she had an extremely intelligent expression for all that, and Mike wondered what deficiency it was in her that caused her to overlook all consideration of her appearance. In the course of his experience he had known many reasons for this, and the commonest one was despair.

At this point in his reflections the door was opened by Jennings to admit a tall girl with smooth red hair and alabaster-white skin. Mrs. Bradley left Mr. Leahy for a moment to welcome her. Then the red-haired girl reached for a drink off Jennings's tray, and came over to Professor Daly. He advanced to greet her with outstretched hands.

"Why, Sodia, how you have grown!" he said, gazing at her with delight.

"It was bound to happen," she said. "Mind my drink."

She held it safely out of reach.

"I had no idea you were going to be here," he said. "Come and meet Mr. Kenny."

Her eyes were emerald green. She was like the Harry Clarke illustration of the Snow Queen, Mike thought. He

45

wondered if his ears had deceived him about her name. Daly introduced her as Miss Milligan.

"You met her father last night," he said. "Professor Milligan. I have the honour to be Sodia's godfather."

He congratulated her on her father's appearance of good health.

"Yes, he's bursting with health," she said. "The only trouble is that the better he feels, the worse grip his little failing has on him. He is a job to look after."

"Still the same?" said Daly sympathetically.

She nodded moodily.

"Of course as long as he doesn't go outside the College he's safe enough. I have got very clever at telling where the things come from."

Mike had stood by, feeling a little embarrassed, though he could only guess at the subject of this conversation. He looked around the room and saw that Professor Burren had come in and was listening superciliously to Mrs. Bradley. The President had gone across to shake hands with a young man who had just slipped into the room, with a quick snake-like movement around the door. He saw Bradley lead him across to Badger, who winced, but then squared his shoulders and made an apparently friendly remark. Bradley signalled with his eyes to Jennings to bring a drink to the latest guest. But Jennings affected not to notice, and bore his tray of drinks right out of the room. Mike noticed that the young man flushed angrily at this and made a snappish remark to Badger.

"Ah-ah!" said Professor Daly's voice in his ear. "It's a very foolish student that talks like that to his professor. Sodia has been telling me about our young friend, but you were staring so hard that you didn't hear."

"What did you call Miss Milligan?" Mike asked urgently.

"Her name is Sylvia, I believe, but her father has always called her Sodia. He says it is easier to remember. She tells me she is paying court to that young man, whose name is Tennyson-Smith, if you can believe that."

He was sulking like a nasty child while she turned an extraordinarily beautiful smile upon him and talked to him eagerly

46

in a low intimate tone. Mike could see that she had the double objective of covering up Tennyson-Smith's bad manners and encouraging him to be happy and enjoy the party. Mike thought enviously how he would burgeon if that smile were ever turned on him. But Tennyson-Smith remained coldly selfish, and even half-turned an insulting shoulder towards her. She flushed quickly and then became absorbed in finishing her drink.

"That fellow is a pup," said Mike angrily.

Daly sighed.

"I tried to tell her she could do better, but it seems he's a Poet, and not only that but a Misunderstood Poet. I'd go bail that I'd understand him, all right!"

"Why is he at this party?" Mike asked.

"He and Sodia are joint secretaries of the Students' Council, she tells me," said Daly. "That could be the reason. But I think it's really because Tennyson-Smith's father is the manager of the College's bank. Bradley's mind always works like that. Tennyson-Smith is not a good sample of student to show to Leahy if that's what Bradley was thinking of. Sodia is fine, though he probably only asked her because she keeps company with him. Bradley doesn't hold much with women——"

Jennings's return to announce dinner interrupted this discourse. Mrs. Bradley moved towards the door, collecting Mrs. Badger and Miss Milligan on the way. The President came next, with an affectionate hand on Tennyson-Smith's arm. His head was turned away, however, to talk to Leahy, who walked at his other side. The young man looked slighted, as well he might, for Bradley was treating him like a child. Mike thought what a strange mistake it was for the President to make, and wondered, not for the first time, whether it might not be a student who had threatened his life. Daly had informed him that the life of a good President is threatened by at least one student every year. For the first time in his life he wished that he had darkened the doors of some university when he was younger.

At dinner Mike sat next to Mrs. Badger. He hardly noticed what he was given to eat, because she questioned him so closely,

47

throughout the meal, about the organization of vocational schools. Every time he tried to change the subject, she hauled him back firmly. She pegged down every statement that he made, and referred back to his former remarks with as much ease as if she had been reading them from a book. All the time that she was talking she ate up her dinner expertly. It was obvious that she deeply enjoyed every bite. Mike looked across at Badger with respect. In his company Mrs. Badger had looked cowed.

Professor Daly was sitting at Bradley's left at the top of the long table. Bradley was fully occupied with Mr. Leahy, who sat at his other side, and Daly had had to content himself with listening to the sour discourse of Burren. He wanted to talk to Badger, but Badger was at the other end of the table, beside Mrs. Bradley. Burren was not a demanding partner. He prosed along about the sins of his colleagues and speared his dinner delicately. If Daly answered him, he paused and lowered his head for a moment and then took up his discourse at the exact point at which he had left off. Daly would have dearly loved to rub Burren's Voltairean nose in his *gâteau à la crème*. Since this was not possible he simply stopped listening to him.

He looked across at Mike who was clearly in difficulties with Mrs. Badger. Daly knew that she was always dangerous when she was savouring temporary freedom from her husband. At any moment, he thought, she would accuse Mike of being the fraud that he was. Now, in the strong ringing tone that he usually kept for the lecture room, Daly called across to Mr. Leahy opposite him:

"Tell us, Mr. Leahy, what exactly are you presenting to the College?"

All conversation stopped, as Daly had intended that it should, and everyone looked fixedly at the little American. He was not at all embarrassed by this. He wiped his mouth with his napkin in a leisurely way and looked around the table.

"We have not exactly decided what it is to be thus far," he said, in the slightly drawling accent which always sounds faintly sardonic to Europeans. "There have been lots of suggestions. A house for the most distinguished professor on the staff was one idea. They have something like that in Copenhagen."

Badger made a strange little choking sound which he smothered in his napkin. Leahy looked down along the table at him, speculatively. Then he went on:

"Yes, the President thought that that would cause trouble, so we abandoned it."

"Comparisons often cause trouble," said Daly quickly.

"Yes," said Leahy. "That's what finished my second idea, too."

"What was that?" asked Burren flatly.

"To develop the most progressive department." The little man moved his shoulders unhappily. "I just want to give something to the College. I don't want to tie it up so that it won't be any use to you. I don't know anything about College—never spent as much as one day there—but your President is a very fine man indeed and I trust him. Yes, sir, I trust him."

"Very nice," said Burren acidly.

Daly restrained himself with difficulty from kicking Burren's shin under the table. Bradley looked as if he were about to stand up and make a speech of thanks. Then Mrs. Bradley broke the tension by saying brightly:

"Oh, you'll think of something, I'm sure. Do have some marshmallows."

Along the table little silver dishes of sweets were ranged. She had them all nibbling by the time the coffee was brought in, a minute later. Bradley had a special little dish, set squarely in front of his own plate, containing a few small, hard biscuits. He reached for them one after another, but he did not offer them to anyone else. Seeing Daly's eye on him, he said:

"I like macaroons. I always have a special dish for myself."

Daly hoped that his expression did not reveal his opinion of Bradley's manners. Burren, at his elbow, snorted and said:

"I like macaroons, too. Could I have one, please?"

He held out his hand for the dish. Bradley gave it to him with a sudden little jerking movement. Burren, looking pleased, took one and bit it in two.

"Delicious!" he said emphatically. "Do have one, Mrs. Badger."

"Thank you," said Mrs. Badger, reaching across the table for the dish.

She held it out to Mike.

"I can guarantee their quality," she said. "The President always has the best of everything."

Mike shook his head, speechless with loathing of the horrible game that they were playing. Down along the table they sent the little dish from one eager hand to the other. Each made a little derisive comment and passed it on with a flourish. Even Miss Milligan and Tennyson-Smith joined in. Daly and Mike avoided each other's eyes. Mr. Leahy looked bewildered. Mrs. Bradley looked frightened. Bradley's face was smooth but his eyes were shadowed with rage and hatred. When Burren handed him back the dish at last, with a single macaroon remaining, he received it without a word. He picked up the biscuit and put it in his mouth as if he were not in the least interested in it. In the midst of an uneasy silence he chewed and swallowed it. Then he stood up and said in a perfectly normal tone:

"Shall we go back to the drawing-room?"

They all pushed back their chairs, a little too noisily, and followed him out of the room.

The rest of the evening was an embarrassing business. Burren was in high good humour now. He kept bursting into little explosions of laughter which were curious to watch, for his features somehow gave the impression that they were not made for laughter. Mrs. Badger talked patronizingly to Mrs. Bradley about foreign travel. Daly found this diverting. He knew that Badger had brought his wife to Paris for their honeymoon and had trailed her, in pitiful high heels, into a succession of the carman's cafés that he had frequented when he had spent a year there on a post-graduate scholarship. Soon all the little Badgers had come along and swallowed up any money that might have served to bring them abroad again.

Mrs. Bradley, on the other hand, had lived in Africa for a number of years, and had spent many summers in French and Italian resorts. Watching how patiently she allowed Mrs. Badger to tell her all about Europe, Daly thought he saw how it was that she had succeeded in living for all these years with Bradley. She was like a pedigree Jersey cow, he thought, small and self-assured and valuable, and as patient as a Buddha. She had not been in the least like this when he had known her, long ago.

Daly sat firmly between Miss Milligan and her young man and devoted himself to making them behave civilly to each other. This took only half of his attention, so that he was able to observe what went on among the other guests. Badger had attached himself to Mike. Daly heard him discoursing on the shortness of life. Once, in a little lull in the general conversation, his voice droned out lugubriously:

"Timor mortis conturbat me."

Mike nodded dumbly, finding no words with which to reply. Burren laughed to himself. Daly wondered how he was going to endure the next hour before they could all decently go home. Bradley and his wife were the only people who seemed to be at ease. The President chatted to Mr. Leahy about the importance of the social side of university life. Mr. Leahy said from time to time:

"Of course I don't know anything at all about College, but I think you're dead right. I think that's mighty important."

He was an abstemious person, Daly noticed. When Jennings brought in a tray with drinks he drank a glass of soda-water. Burren looked sharply at the labels and said:

"Ha! Tullamore Dew!"

He poured himself a half tumblerful, put a single splash of soda-water into it, and drank it all within five minutes, without any visible effect. Miss Milligan had whiskey, too.

"Do you like it?" Professor Daly asked.

"I need it," she said sharply. "And for heaven's sake don't preach about it——"

"I wasn't going to," said Daly, "but now I will. Young women who drink whiskey with enjoyment are taking the risk of pickling their insides beyond repair, and of ending their lives in the company of little green men only four inches high."

"The last part of it would be rather nice," she retorted, with a sidelong glare at Tennyson-Smith.

51

Daly would have expected the young man to pour himself some whiskey, too, but he had a bottle of lager. Mike Kenny miserably refused all consolation. Daly wondered if Badger could possibly have converted him to his view of the world. Bradley had not spoken to Mike since dinner had finished, but he glanced across at him from time to time as if to make sure that Mike was watching the guests as he had been asked to do.

It was Leahy who broke up the party at last. He looked at his watch and stood up.

"You'll excuse me, President," he said. "I aim to be in bed by ten-thirty. It's now just on ten. I've had a most enjoyable evening. You think over the whole proposition some more. There must be some good way to spend fifty thousand dollars."

He shook hands with each member of the party. Daly noticed that he had each person's name correctly. The President went out of the room with Leahy. Burren watched the door close and then opened his mouth to speak. Just in time, however, he glanced quickly at Mrs. Bradley and sank back in his chair again. Professor Daly stood up firmly and said:

"It's time that I went home, too. I have my first lecture in the morning and even now at this hour of my life, I find that disturbing."

"Lecturing never bothered me," said Burren, with a snort.

"I worry a lot about it, I must confess," said Badger. "It's terrible to think how a lightly spoken word of mine might send an innocent young person to perdition."

"Surely you never speak lightly," said Burren rudely.

Fortunately Bradley returned just then. Now he seemed to have forgotten the strained little scene in the dining-room, and to be held in a sort of glow of pleasure in Leahy and his money.

"Yes, he is the most normal of them all," said Daly to himself.

This reflection made him rather sad, because when he had been one of them he had not thought them odd at all. His changed point of view was a measure of the gap that had developed between himself and his old colleagues.

Bradley ignored the expectant looks turned upon him and

52

made no reference whatever to Mr. Leahy. He shook hands with everyone and led them all towards the door, with a light hand on Professor Burren's shoulder. He did not seem to notice how Burren winced and shrank away from him. In a little fever of embarrassment, Daly tried to divert the President's attention to himself. He said that he would like to see over the buildings next day for old time's sake. Bradley turned to him, dropping his hand from Burren's shoulder. Burren crossed the hall away from him with a strangely expressive wriggling movement of disgust. Daly wondered why Burren had accepted an invitation to dine at the President's house at all, since he hated him so much.

"I'll come over to your rooms at two o'clock," Bradley was saying, "and we'll go about together. You'll be busy with your lecture in the morning. I won't be able to get to it, I'm afraid, but Badger will look after you."

When the door had shut behind them Burren said a general curt: "Good night!" and marched off across the quadrangle. Tennyson-Smith got his hand under his true love's elbow and dragged her away with him. Mrs. Badger, who seemed to have become deeply attached to Mike Kenny, pressed him to come and visit their sett the next time that he was in town. Professor Badger suggested lugubriously that Daly should lie awake all night worrying as to whether his first lecture would or would not be a success. Then they were gone, pattering off along the gravel, clutched together because of the darkness.

5

Left alone with the old man Inspector Kenny gave vent to a short, sharp howl of laughter.

"Stop that!" said Daly. "Come over to my place. I have a bottle of whiskey."

"It's just that I never met such people before," said Mike apologetically. "Are there many like Mrs. Badger about?"

"Not many," said Daly. "I must show you some of the other kind to-morrow."

"To-morrow!" Mike groaned. "Must I come again to-morrow?"

"You promised," said Daly. "Don't be so hide-bound. You should value the opportunity of seeing how people live in universities."

"I do value it," said Mike humbly, "but I can't like it."

He felt more cheerful after he had had a glass of Daly's whiskey, which was quite as good as Bradley's. Daly stirred up the wood fire. Its warmth was pleasant after the October chill of the night outside. Mike complained for a few minutes, without interruption, about the deception into which he had been forced. At last Daly said:

"For heaven's sake stop worrying about that. After all, you were not deceiving your host. I would have had some sympathy with you if you had to do that. The rest of them don't care what your profession is. They were all thinking of themselves, every one of them."

"That is true," said Mike. "Still, I was a wolf in sheep's clothing——"

"Wolf!" said the old man. "You are a sheep in sheep's clothing! Where's your detective spirit, man?"

"Um," said Mike.

54

"What did you think of Leahy?" Daly asked.

"The answer to Bradley's prayer, I should say," said Mike. "Bradley could do what he likes with that money, as far as I can see."

"Short of keeping a few thousand pounds for himself just for being a good boy," said Daly.

"He seems to be very wealthy," said Mike. After a pause he went on: "That was a disgraceful scene about the macaroons."

"I had not thought them capable of it," said Daly, half to himself. "Even Sodia——"

He sighed deeply.

Presently Mike stood up to go home, promising to come to Daly's lecture in the morning. He said that he would try to arrange for leave to spend the day in the College.

"But the President has not asked for help," he said uneasily, "and really I have nothing to show them——"

"Tell them you'll have Bradley's body to show them if they don't let you come," said Daly brutally.

The President's house was in darkness when Mike passed it on his way down the avenue. He promised himself that he would call there to-morrow immediately after Daly's lecture, and ask Bradley to discuss the whole affair with him. A clever man would surely see that it was nonsense at this stage to have Daly as an intermediary. The line of thought started by this reflection kept him occupied all the way back to his lodgings.

It was five minutes to noon when he reached the College next day. He had found it surprisingly hard to convince his superiors that his presence was necessary to save the President's life. They had released him at last, however, with the stipulation that it was to be for one day only. If there were no developments at the College by the evening he was to go back to his ordinary work. Seven more of those forged notes had come in, his superior said pettishly. That was far more important than playing watchdog to some silly man who was afraid of the dark.

In the main hall Jennings was waiting to conduct him to the scene of Daly's lecture. This was a long room, well lighted with oblong Georgian windows, and furnished as a library with

55

chairs and long, leather-covered tables. The walls were lined with glass-fronted book-shelves. Mike took his place at the end of the room, behind the already assembled audience.

There were about two hundred people present. They sat at the tables, looking towards the top of the room, where there was a little dais for the lecturer. The fact that they were not placed in rows gave the whole business a pleasing air of informality. Mike thought that Daly would like this. The outsiders, recognizable by their overcoats, their hats and their age, had congregated near the dais, with earnest expressions and notebooks at the ready. Mike found himself surrounded by students, male and female. Their penetrating, all-seeing eyes frightened him, so that he shrank against the bookcase behind him. Tennyson-Smith was there with Sodia, as Mike had begun to call her in his mind. They seemed a little more pleased with each other's company this morning. Tennyson-Smith had fixed a wicked eye on the lecturer's chair. Mike's practice as observer at political meetings told him that the young man was planning to heckle. He felt quite sorry for him. There would be small satisfaction indeed in heckling Professor Daly.

Intent as he was on watching Tennyson-Smith, he had not noticed a young man leave his place at the other side of the room and come to sit in the vacant chair beside his own, until a voice said genially:

"May the harp of old Ireland never want for a string as long as there's a gut in a policeman!"

Mike felt a tremor run through him. He turned to greet the young man with a warning frown, and said in a low voice:

"Keep quiet, Johnny. Don't tell the world who I am."

"Don't call me Johnny!" the young man spluttered. "I've just trained everyone to say John." He sat down and peered at Mike with lively interest. "Are you travelling *infra dig*?"

"More or less," said Mike. "What are you doing here yourself?"

"Pursuing the Arts," said John. "Surely your fellows in Galway have noticed by now that I disappear mysteriously three times a year?"

"They probably haven't got you on their books yet," said

56

Mike mildly. "Why don't you pursue the Arts in Galway, you little traitor?"

"I'd like it better," said John, "but my mother says she needs a rest. Awfully selfish of her, don't you think?"

"Dreadful," said Mike. "I had noticed that you were developing a metropolitan polish. Now don't go telling anyone about me, young Johnny, or I'll rub your nose in the mud!"

"There's a return for my kindly interest!" said John.

He marched back to his former seat. Mike heard one of his friends ask:

"Who is your buddy, John?"

"A plumber looking for culture," said John airily. "It will probably knock him right off his drain-pipe. Great mistake this mass education."

Just then a door at the top of the room opened, and a little procession came in. Professor Badger was in front, head down, and with the weight of the world on his bent shoulders. Next came Daly, smiling genially about, with the simple pleasure of a prima donna. After him came Professor Fox. Mike was surprised to see him there, until he remembered that he was the registrar. Fox looked bored, as indeed he probably was. The extern members of the audience clapped slightly, while all three sat down. Then Badger stood up again and moved forward with an appearance of weariness to introduce the lecturer.

He spoke for twenty minutes without a break, swaying slightly from heel to toe and never once lifting his eyes from his ill-polished shoes. He recalled his younger days when Daly had opened the vast doors of English literature to him. He said that Daly had inspired not only Badger but every sane member of his class to the writing of English. He named Daly's five celebrated students and a whole covey of minor ones that no one had ever heard of, but that Badger swore made their living by the pen. He said that the world was in a parlous state, and that it was beyond hope that people like Daly could save it by their petty potterings at culture. He said that the only fate in store for himself and the entire audience was to give up all hope of fulfilment or achievement, come to terms with frustration and creep about to find themselves dishonourable graves. He called up Nietzsche and Sartre to support him, with accurate quotations. At last he sat down, sank his head on his chest and appeared to fall into a gloomy sleep.

Hearing a snort behind him Mike turned to see that Burren and one or two other professors had come in during Badger's discourse. The students' eyes sparkled, but they gave no other sign of the awful joy that must have swelled their susceptible souls to bursting-point. When Professor Daly stood up they stamped their feet gently to show their appreciation. But then they waited, as civilly as the outsiders, for him to begin.

Three minutes later Badger was forgotten. Mike had often heard of Daly's skill and power as a lecturer. Now as he listened he began to understand something of the reason why the students stopped grinning, the outsiders' notebooks slipped unheeded into their laps, and even the professors forgot to look as if they knew it all before. Tennyson-Smith's jaw, always highly flexible, dropped open and hung thus throughout the lecture, so that a wandering fly could easily have buzzed in and out of his mouth, if it had so wished.

Daly's thesis was simple. He began by thanking Badger for reminding them of the present parlous state of the world. He rolled the adjective pleasurably on his tongue. When external conditions were so terrible, the life of the mind assumed a greater importance. Anyone can live happily in Paradise, he said. It takes a clever man to live happily in hell.

"Tut-tut!" said a parson at the front table.

Thus, Daly went on undisturbed, it behoved every man who wanted to shape the destiny of the world with his pen, to pause and think which was the more powerful, the weeping or the laughter. He urged them to create a world of the mind which would eventually influence the physical world and change it. For half a century, he said, he had devoted himself to the task of getting the starkness out of Anglo-Irish literature. He implored them to stop writing about undigested alcohol and drains. He implored them not to go to the other extreme and write about primroses and lambkins, either, if they did not wish to inflict their readers with wool-ball. Seen from the right

58

point of view, he said, even love and marriage were not without their lighter moments.

Mike wondered at the way in which Daly seemed to have foreseen exactly how long he could hold the attention of his audience. He bounced them along from point to point of his discourse, leaving them increasingly breathless but still eager. Mike saw the fire of fiction slowly dawning in their eyes. Now hot, shaky hands were fumbling for pencils with which to note great thoughts. But there was only time for a word before they were swept on again. The students's ears, always prominent, seemed to have increased in size, so ardently were they stretched in the lecturer's direction. There was not a sound as the old man gathered up the ends of his arguments and tied them into a reef knot. Even when he had finished the silence continued until he had sat down. Then someone gave a little sigh, and a moment later there was a storm of applause from the students.

Badger shook himself awake and looked around him. A voice on Mike's right called out derisively:

"False alarm, Badger! Winter's not over yet!"

It was Mike's friend, John Fahy. Some of his friends hustled him outside, while the others redoubled their cheers. Badger stood up and waved a feeble hand for order. Fox, who had shown no sign of interest until now, was seen to glance sharply about and note a name or two on the paper in front of him. Silence fell.

"Professor Daly's next lecture will be given at noon on Monday," droned Badger. "The subject will be 'The Crafty Novelist'——"

He glanced sideways with annoyance at a porter who had come in and was whispering agitatedly to Fox. It was Jennings. Mike saw Daly's face go white. He waited for no more. He leaped to his feet and pushed his way without ceremony through the little crowd around the door. Outside in the lobby he paused for a second. Then he saw a passageway running by the side of the lecture-room. Darting along it he reached the top just as Daly, Jennings, Fox and Badger came out of the library by the upper door. Fox had tears in his eyes. Mike grasped Jennings's arm.

"What's the matter?"

"It's a matter for the College, sir," said Jennings with dignity.

"He's a policeman, Jennings," said Daly wearily. "Mike, Bradley is dead, after all."

6

"A policeman?" said Jennings sharply. "What's a policeman doing here? I don't like the look of this at all, Professor, and I don't mind telling you——"

"Mr. Kenny is a friend of mine," said Daly soothingly. "He has just been at my lecture. We're very fortunate in having him here to help us. He understands this kind of thing."

"What kind of thing?" Jennings persisted. "What do we want with the police? The President died in the night the way any of us might. Why did you say he's dead 'after all'? I want to know that, so I do!"

"Slip of the tongue," said Daly, coldly fixing a hard eye on Jennings. "This is no longer your responsibility, Jennings, and I should advise you not to take too much upon yourself."

They measured each other. Then Jennings looked a little uncomfortable and said:

"All right, sir, so long as there's someone in charge."

He looked meaningly at Fox, who seemed suddenly to recollect himself as he said:

"Yes, yes, I'm in charge, I suppose. We'd better not stand here. Shall we go over to the President's Lodging? Yes, that would be best."

People were pouring out of the library now. They had sensed that something was wrong. One or two professors, headed by Burren, began to walk purposefully along the passageway towards the little group. Jennings hissed:

"This way, gentlemen!"

He led them out by another door into the quadrangle. They crossed it quickly and had reached the President's Lodging just as the first students emerged from the library entrance. They were admitted immediately by an extremely intelligent-looking parlourmaid of uncertain years. Daly thanked Jennings gravely and left him standing, surprised, outside on the steps. Fox said abstractedly:

"What's all this, Nellie? What's all this?"

She was impeccably dressed and showed no sign of agitation except that her frilled, starched apron had moved to the back. Daly put out a thoughtful hand and pulled it around to the front again. She stroked it absently, as a cat might lick a returned kitten.

Mike took her attention by asking if Mrs. Bradley could be seen.

"I gave her two aspirins and made her lie down, sir," said Nellie. "It was a nasty shock for her."

"Come into the study and tell us all about it," said Daly, who always hated standing about in halls.

The study was like a stage setting, expectant but somehow painfully lonely. The firelight reflected on the polished furniture and the bright autumn garden beyond the windows only served to heighten this impression, so that Daly had to pause on the threshold to recover himself before moving on into the room. Fox was snuffling again. Then he remembered that he had a handkerchief, and blew his nose with a trumpeting sound. No one sat down. The armchairs looked too deep and comfortable and the only straight chair was Bradley's own, placed before his desk. No one wanted to sit in that. Daly took up a stand with his back to the fire and said kindly:

"Now, Nellie, tell us all about it."

"I think I'll wait outside," said Fox. "I'm a little upset."

Nellie looked appealingly after him as he went out, as if she did not like to be abandoned to the other two.

"I don't know anything, really, sir," she said hurriedly. "We only found him a little while ago."

"Why was that?" asked Mike. "It's after one o'clock now."

She seemed pleased to be given a starting-point for her story.

"The President usually got up at about eight o'clock," she said, "but now and then he'd take a notion to sleep on. He was a terrible cross man, God rest him. We usen't go near him until he'd ring the bell for a cup of tea when he'd wake up."

"Did he sometimes sleep until midday?" asked Daly.

"No, no, sir. Never. Always about ten o'clock he'd get up. That's why we got uneasy about him this morning, when it was so late."

"How was it you didn't go in at about eleven?" Daly persisted. "That would have been an hour beyond his usual time."

"I was afraid," said Nellie simply. "And I was polishing up the furniture in here, too, while I had the chance. I didn't want to bring him out on top of me sooner than I had to."

Mike sighed.

"It's a pity you picked this morning for a special clean-up," he said mildly. "Try to remember if there was anything unusual about the room."

Nellie wrinkled her forehead.

" 'Twas the same as it always was after a party," she said. "The President used always to bring anyone he wanted to talk to private in here, and there would be glasses, and ashtrays around. 'Twas the same as usual."

"How many glasses had been used?"

"I think two, but I wouldn't like to swear to it. With all the excitement it's gone out of my head."

"And was there nothing strange, nothing at all?"

Mike hoped he did not sound too pressing, for he had more than once encountered witnesses who were so anxious to please that they had made up a story rather than see him disappointed.

"Look around the room slowly and you may remember if anything was out of place."

She stretched her neck while she did so, as if to help her to see further. At last she said:

"There wasn't anything, unless maybe the ticket."

"What ticket?"

"I put it under the blotter." She went over to the desk and lifted the leather-covered blotter. A small piece of blue paper, printed in black, lay underneath. "Here it is, sir."

It was a ticket for a symphony concert which was to take place in the first week in November.

"What is strange about that?" Mike asked.

"Nothing," said Nellie, a little huffily, "except that it was

63

lying on the floor by the desk. I was only trying to remember anything out of the way——"

Mike soothed her down and thanked her for her help and presently she went on:

"That ticket wasn't on the floor when I brought in the tray of drinks at nine o'clock. I'll swear to that. I'd have seen it and picked it up if it had been."

Mike was folding the ticket and putting it into his pocket as he said:

"And Mrs. Bradley! Where was she?"

"She has her own room, next to the President's," said Nellie. "I brought her breakfast at half-past eight, as usual, and she got up a while after. She went into town at ten o'clock. When she came back I told her the President wasn't up yet. 'Twas herself opened the door and went in. I heard her calling out, and I ran in to her, and there he was in bed, in the dark, with the curtains pulled and him stone cold dead. The poor man. I never liked him, but you'd be kind of sorry for a person when you'd see them dead," she finished thoughtfully.

"So you told Jennings?" said Daly quickly.

"That's right, sir. I told him to find someone responsible and tell them, and while he was gone I got Mrs. Bradley to lie down. That's all I could do."

"You didn't move him, I suppose?"

"I did not," said Nellie. "I shut out the door and locked it, the way no one would go in. That Annie down in the kitchen is a proper little ghoul—she thinks we're all going to die except herself. I wouldn't put it past her to be peeping in at him when my back was turned." She paused and looked worriedly at Daly. "I didn't send for the priest, sir. The President never went to Mass, church nor meeting."

Suddenly there were tears in her eyes.

"It's hard to do everything right, so it is."

"You've been wonderfully good," said Daly soothingly. "Now just show us the President's room. We'll look after everything else."

She led them out into the hall. Unlike Jennings she showed no resentment of Mike's presence. Mike was glad of this, for he did not wish to spread the news of his profession just yet. Fox had made no comment upon it. But Fox looked dazed just now. He hung back as they went upstairs, and almost seemed to be considering running away. While Nellie was unlocking the door of Bradley's bedroom he was moving slowly along the corridor. While they were inside he stood uncertainly at the door.

Mike was pleased about this, for he was always disturbed by the presence of emotional laymen at the scene of a murder. Professor Daly he almost regarded as a partner. Still, he glanced anxiously at the old man as they crossed to the huge luxurious bed where Bradley lay, and wondered whether it would have been wiser to have made him stay outside.

Five minutes later, when they locked the door behind them again and stood facing each other in the corridor, Daly looked pale and shocked. Fox had wandered away to the other end of the corridor and was gazing out on to the quadrangle. Mike grasped Daly's arm and said in a low voice, so that Fox should not hear:

"Don't take it so hard. It was not nice, but you won't see it again."

"Sorry," said Daly, with a feeble grin. "It was that blue colour of his skin—I did not expect it."

"Yes," said Mike, half to himself, "one clings to the notion that he might have died naturally, in his sleep. But I'm afraid there is no question of that."

"I have heard that there are some heart conditions that turn the skin blue at death," said Daly uncertainly, "but then we must not forget the——"

"Yes, you must forget," said Mike earnestly. "Leave all that to the experts. It's no use speculating when you have no scientific knowledge."

He was pleased to see the old man revive a little as he said:

"There is plenty to speculate about, apart from the cause of his death. I wish you had known Bradley better. Then you would perhaps better be able to estimate whether he was capable of suicide."

Though Mike had not excluded this possibility, he affected

65

an air of surprise which made Daly preen himself a little and even smile in a somewhat superior way as he said:

"Oh, yes, in spite of the threats to his life, we must think of suicide. For one thing, we only have Bradley's word for it that he received those threats. Professors and university people in general are a race apart," he went on seriously. "After a number of years of concentration on the abstract, they tend to lose touch with reality. You have seen how sensitive they are. They can make a full-scale grievance out of something that a business man would hardly notice. To me it does not seem impossible that a professor wishing to commit suicide would first build up a story about anonymous letters and threats, so as to give himself the necessary impetus to carry out his wish for death."

While the old man discoursed they had been moving towards the head of the stairs. Fox joined them there, and listened sceptically to his last sentence. Daly, now quite recovered, turned to him eagerly and said:

"Don't you agree with me, Fox? It's very important that Mike should understand——"

"I think you're talking rubbish," said Fox rudely. "Bradley was the most sensible, down-to-earth man I ever met. He would never have thought it necessary to deceive himself like that."

"Like what?" asked Mike innocently.

"Faking all that stuff about anonymous letters," said Fox, staring. "They were no fake. I saw them."

"You did?" exclaimed Daly. "When?"

"A couple of weeks ago. He showed them to me."

They walked downstairs in silence. Daly was thinking how like Bradley it was to have refused to show him the letters, when he had already shown them to Fox and possibly to several other people as well. It was as if, having employed Daly, he was not going to help him in any way lest he make his task easier. Since one of Daly's own maxims was that one should not hire a dog and bark oneself, he could not but experience a little fellow-feeling with Bradley. Still his resentment was undoubtedly based on the fact that he had insisted on acting as a friend to Bradley, and not as an employee.

66

"But where's the use," he said to himself. "He's dead now, so my status doesn't matter."

Through the open door the study seemed full of people.

"I'll go and telephone," said Mike. "You go in there and tell them what has happened."

Nellie came scuttling from the back of the hall, hissing conspiratorially:

"I couldn't keep them out, sir. They just walked straight in. They said they wanted to see Mrs. Bradley, but I haven't called her, the poor creature——"

"Quite right, Nellie," said Daly. "I'll see them myself." He paused in the doorway and watched them for a second before they noticed him. Badger was there, clearly possessed of a sort of gloomy excitement that kept him walking up and down like the black leopard in the adjoining zoo. He was looking at his feet, as he always did when he wished to conceal his thoughts. Little Hamilton, looking somehow all wrong without his smile, was darting penetrating glances about at his colleagues, with terrifying professorial detachment. Milligan was in an elevated mood. Daly saw him slip a silver ashtray off the desk into his pocket, as he chatted animatedly with Miss O'Leary. She was the only one of the group who seemed to realize the presence of tragedy. An intelligent woman, Daly thought. Even in his agitation his eyes rested in quiet momentary contemplation on her beauty, as a dragon-fly rests on a still pool. She looked up suddenly and saw him and started across the room.

"Thank heavens you're here!" she said without ceremony. "What on earth is happening? That beastly Jennings just said the President is dead and the police are in. Is it true? We're all longing to know."

By the time she had finished there was silence in the room. Burren, who since he had noticed Daly had been affecting to study the titles of books on the shelves, now rambled across with his hands in his pockets. Delaney hovered at the fireplace with a painfully eager cock of the head so as to miss nothing. Fox slipped into the room behind Daly and shut the door.

"Yes, Bradley is dead," said Daly. "We have just seen him. Inspector Kenny thinks he had been poisoned."

67

"I don't believe it," said Delaney testily. "Bradley would never take poison. I once knew a man who committed suicide and he was not in the least like Bradley. Not in the least."

"No one said Bradley committed suicide," said Miss O'Leary, turning her sharp blue gaze on Delaney. "I take it that someone gave him poison."

"Did you hear what she said?" Delaney spluttered shrilly. "She's saying I poisoned him! Stop looking at me, woman! I had nothing to do with it! I know you want to get rid of me, but you should have some notion of where to stop——"

"I did not say you poisoned him," Miss O'Leary interrupted in a loud, ringing voice.

Burren laughed sourly, glancing from one of them to the other. Feeling pleased that Mike was absent, Daly intervened:

"Please let us not quarrel. We are all certain to have a few difficult days. The police will be considerate. There is no cause for alarm——"

"I am not alarmed," said Burren.

"Nor am I," said Badger truculently.

Though they hated to be called to order, Daly could see that his words had had the effect he wanted of restoring something like normality. Fox was saying, in a new tone of authority:

"Now, we must make a point of having everything continue as if there were nothing wrong. The students may get out of hand if we're not careful. Break up big groups if you see them, and do not give any information——"

"I think it would be much better to issue a statement of some kind," said Miss O'Leary.

"We'll call a meeting then," said Fox hurriedly. "We must appoint an acting President."

"Ha!" said Badger.

In despair, Daly saw all their hackles rise again. But at that moment the door opened and Mike put his head in, cautiously:

"Come along, Mike," said Daly, too heartily. He turned in a sort of sweep to the others. "This is Inspector Kenny, an old friend of mine. We're very fortunate in having him——"

Out of the corner of his eye he saw Milligan replace the ash-tray on the desk. Delaney took a little running step forward.

"No, no, no!" he said querulously. "That is the man we all met the other night. He's a vocational school teacher from somewhere in the west. Don't you remember?"

He looked up solicitously into Daly's face. Mike grinned wryly at the company. He saw Miss O'Leary's eyes narrow. Then she said:

"There is more in this than meets the eye. If you really are a policeman," Mike nodded, "then we had better go away and leave you in peace. Professor Daly will show you where to find us when you want us. Come along, everyone."

And she herded them, in masterly fashion, right out of the house. Delaney and Milligan looked back over their shoulders once or twice, like small boys who want to stay and watch a fire, but she would not allow them as much as one question. At the front door, just before she closed it, she turned and gave Daly and Mike a broad and expert wink. Mike started, shocked. It was as if the Mona Lisa, hanging decorously in her chaste frame, had winked at him. He followed Daly back into the study and closed the door mechanically. Then he asked:

"Who is she?"

"Professor O'Leary," said Daly severely. "Don't forget what you know about professors, *all* professors. And I would no more think of having her about the house than I would a jungle tiger."

"Some people do keep tigers," said Mike feebly.

"For a little while only," said Daly meaningly. "Have you sent for reinforcements?"

"Yes, they are on their way." He shook his head regretfully. "Police doctor coming, too." He sighed. "I suppose you're right about the tiger."

Twenty minutes later they were so deep in conversation that they did not hear the doorbell ring. Nellie came into the room, still scuttling and whispering.

"There's three men in the hall. Big, huge men with water-proofs." She sketched their dimensions in the air. "What will I say to them? And that Jennings has got in with them, sir. I didn't see him until he was inside the house."

"I'll settle him," said Daly grimly. "To work, Mike!"

Mike, who had dropped into an armchair only a moment before, now unfolded his long body with a sigh and heaved himself upright again. Then they followed Nellie out into the hall.

7

They found Jennings cowered against the closed front door, transfixed by the speculative quiet eyes of the three huge men in waterproofs. When he saw Daly he slipped around them and ran forward.

"I'm not doing anything, sir!" he said with indignant rage. "Tell them to stop looking at me. I only came to say that I asked the restaurant to keep lunch for yourself and—and *them*, if you're late."

"That was good of you, Jennings," said Daly gravely. "We'll all be along later."

Jennings did not appear to trust himself to reach the front door in safety, for he backed down the hall until he could open the service door and dart through.

"What did you do to him, MacCarthy?" asked Mike.

"We just looked at him," said one of the giants. "A bit closely, I'll admit. Then we sort of nodded to each other. That was all."

They nodded solemnly, to show how it was done.

"It seems to have silenced Jennings, anyway," said Daly with satisfaction.

Mike introduced two of them as Sergeant MacCarthy and Guard Murphy. The third man, though he seemed identical with the others, turned out to be the doctor. His name was Mullen.

"There's great excitement below in the office," said Sergeant MacCarthy, looking pleased. "The boss seems to think you bumped off the President yourself. He says it's a mighty queer thing how you knew in advance what was going to happen."

"Very funny," said Mike coldly. "Come along upstairs, Doctor. You two can come also, for one look. Then you can start working out where everyone of the hundreds of people who inhabit this College spent the last twenty-four hours!"

He marched off up the stairs, followed briskly by the doctor, and somewhat more slowly by the other two. Daly waited uncertainly in the hall, until they had gone out of sight around the turn of the stairs. Then he went back into the study and stood on the hearthrug looking into the fire. He was not a nervous man, but in the next few minutes he felt a sort of compulsion grow from the air about him, palpably forcing him to go out of the room. In spite of the fire the air seemed to have become clammy and cold. A sudden flurry of wind swept up through the sunny garden and rattled the window-panes. Behind him he imagined that a moulded fog had grown to towering size and would overwhelm him at any moment.

"So that is the sort of man you were," he said softly. "A cold, cold man, with a cold ghost."

But having pronounced the word he found that he could not stay for another moment. He turned swiftly, but cautiously. He was by no means reassured at finding the room empty. He gave the late President's chair a wide berth—did it move a little as he fluttered past?—and reached for the door-knob with a sweating hand. Outside in the hall courage swept back to him again so that he was able to hold the door open for a moment and say:

"Sorry, old boy. I didn't know you wanted to be alone." And then, meditatively, as he shut the door with a little click: "Should I lose you living and vex you dead?"

He was relieved to find the hall empty. He did not wish to shatter Nellie's nerves by telling her to whom he had been talking. Still he would have felt he owed it to himself to do so, if she had been a bewildered spectator of his emergence from the study. He let himself out of the front door and stopped in astonishment.

Usually at this hour the quadrangle was deserted. It was not yet two o'clock, and most of the students and staff should have been at luncheon, except for the few odd souls who liked to lecture at one. To-day, however, when he turned around from closing the door, Daly found himself looking into hundreds of

72

pairs of eyes, all sparkling with fiendish anticipation. Though he could see some other people as well, most of them were students, close-packed and single-minded as a crowd waiting for the arrival of Mr. de Valera. In that first moment it occurred to Daly that this was why Bradley's ghost had urged him to come out. It had wanted him to restore order. All Presidents, he reflected delightedly, even dead ones, hate to see students congregate in large crowds.

From his little elevation on the steps of the President's Lodging, Daly was able to see across the heads of the crowd to the far side of the quadrangle. His eyesight was not good, so that it was a moment or two before he recognized the figure that was moving agitatedly up and down behind the unconcerned backs of the farthermost students. It was Fox, and he was plainly engaged in trying to disperse the crowd by individual persuasion. They took no more notice of him than if he had been a hawker at a hurling match. With Daly's arrival they had pressed forward a little more. Now all conversation ceased. Clearly he was expected to make a speech, newly come as he was from the scene of the drama.

His eyes narrowed thoughtfully. Then he spoke in a casual tone, but loud enough to carry to the farthest limits of his audience.

"There can scarcely be one of us who has not at some time come upon the scene of a street accident. As we walk towards it we become aware of a group of curiously uninhibited persons, standing on their toes to see over each other's heads, necks outstretched, mouths open, all other purposes forgotten in the one delight of observing at first hand the blood and misfortune of a fellow-man. Someone—I forget for the moment who it was—has written a short story in which he propounds a thesis that these *rubbernecks* are always the same people, who hurry from one accident to another with religious devotion. They never offer help. They just stare. Usually they are silent, but there was one celebrated occasion when they sang to keep themselves amused during a long vigil. That was while they waited for the hanging of one Mrs. Manning, poor soul, who had so far forgotten herself as to murder someone—was it

73

her husband? Perhaps you would know." A slightly harder note crept into his voice as he went on: "Perhaps you would like to sing? You may have to wait a long time. It will be dull for you, standing there——"

But by this time the crowd, red-faced and shuffling angrily, had begun to disperse. Those on the edges were fortunate in being able to pretend that they had suddenly met friends with whom they longed to talk, or that they had stopped to admire the fine view of the park from the quadrangle. The middle of the crowd and especially those who had been to the front, concentrated on getting outside the range of Daly's discomfiting eye with all possible speed. He did not move until most of them were gone, but stood there unsmiling and inscrutable. At last he stepped down on to the path and began to walk slowly towards the main door.

Before he could reach it he saw Professor O'Leary come from the direction of the library and hurry towards him.

"You brute!" she said, as soon as she was near enough. "You have shattered the ego of every student in this College."

"Yes," said Daly complacently. "My tongue has not lost its cunning. And you'll find that the egos will recover like the daisies, cut down yet up again as blithe as ever."

"You have a heart of stone," said she admiringly.

"I am seventy-four years old," said Daly, "and I can say exactly what I please. You have no idea of the joy of that. But I must confess that that performance just now cost me a little effort. Walk about with me a little, Mary, if you're not going somewhere else."

"Of course," she said quickly.

Though she knew him long enough not to be deceived by his pathetic tone, still she always found herself responding to it.

"Tell me, how are people taking the news?" he asked eagerly, as they walked slowly around the quadrangle.

"Just as you saw. There is an air of rather callous excitement. All work is suspended, of course, except by Donovan. He is giving a lecture on assassinations, the students tell me. He began with the origin of the word and its ancient practice.

74

They thought he was drunk because he said 'hashshashin'. Then he discoursed on confidence-trick assassinations, as in Nelson's method with General Caracciolo, and the more subtle Borgia style as opposed to the common behind-the-ditch variety. He has not even got to Sarajevo yet, and he *says* he is going to finish with some remarks on the psychological effects of assassinations. That will be late to-night, as far as I can judge. Most of his class has slipped out and he has not even noticed."

"But who is listening to all this?" asked Daly.

"Four Christian Brothers, in the front row," said Mary. "They are writing down every word and they are far too polite to go away. It seems to be an inspired lecture."

She glanced sideways at Daly, who said calmly:

"Inspired with his delight in Bradley's death, I suppose. That is the general feeling, without a doubt. I'm afraid that Mike is going to have a difficult time."

"You think that one of us did in the President?" she said eagerly. "Certainly some of us were behaving very oddly. There's Milligan, who pinched a sugar-castor out of the restaurant just now and had to be pursued by Denny to get it back. Do stay with that policeman," she said earnestly. "You'll be able to explain things to him."

Just then Fox came bustling towards them. As he came near Daly could see that he was almost in a state of hysteria. He clutched an arm of each of them and said earnestly, peering into Daly's face:

"I can never thank you enough for getting that mob to break up. I was in despair. I mean, they just would not *go* for me. I always used to be able for them, but to-day—I suppose it was the shock of all this—poor Bradley——"

"Come and have lunch with me, Foxy," said Miss O'Leary. "There's nothing like food for settling the nerves."

"Do you know, I'm quite hungry," said Fox in surprise. "Perhaps that is what I need."

She led him away towards the restaurant. As he started back to the President's Lodging, Daly reflected on the pleasure of being rescued twice in one day by such an enchanting champion.

75

"God be with the youth of me!" he said to himself with a mournful shake of the head. He knew now that it was selfish jealousy that had impelled him to warn Mike against the dangers of keeping a tame tiger.

He found Mike and Mullen in Bradley's hall. The doctor was pulling on his gloves, breathing loudly like a groom, as doctors often do when they are faced with sudden death.

"Mullen says that he was poisoned all right," said Mike. "Go on, Mullen."

"Nitro-benzene, I think," said Mullen.

Daly made a little exclamation, which he smothered quickly into a question:

"What is that?"

"Nitric acid on benzene," said Mullen. "It smells like almonds. It is used to perfume hair-oil and in flavourings. I once saw a fellow who had died of drinking his hair oil. Rather like drinking one's bath-water, don't you think? That is how I recognized what had happened to our friend upstairs. There is the characteristic blue colour of the skin——"

"Don't tell us!" said Daly sharply. "I don't want to know."

"Thought you were interested," said Mullen coolly. "Well, I'll be moving on, Kenny. There's a butcher in Fairview has just cloven his assistant to the breeches belt. You'll see about the post-mortem?"

He shook hands weakly with Daly and let himself out, whistling the "Marseillaise" metallically through his teeth. Daly looked after him with dislike, but he made no comment. Mike said:

"Come into the study. MacCarthy and Murphy are there. We need your help."

They found the two policemen standing poised for departure just inside the door.

"I thought you were never coming, sir," said the sergeant. "Me stomach thinks me throat is cut."

"There will be a meal for us in the restaurant," said Daly, "but, please, if you must tell me about the doctor's report, do it now, not over a meal."

"There is nothing to tell yet," said Mike, with a calculating

76

eye on Daly. "We must have a post-mortem, as you heard Mullen say. If it is nitro-benzene, as he suggests, he told me one or two interesting things about it. First, that it is a slow-acting poison, and that Bradley could have taken it at any time from six o'clock last evening onwards. Second, that death can be caused by the victim's inhaling the vapour of nitro-benzene. Third, that the taking of alcohol with nitro-benzene accelerates its action. Fourth, that nitro-benzene is heavy and would lie at the bottom of the glass, allowing the poisoner to drink the top to prove his good faith."

"Stop!" shouted Daly, who had been slowly coming to the boil during this discourse. "You are a deadly bore, Mike. And if I were you I'd arrest the doctor. He seems to know far too much about it." He walked unhappily across the room. "Now I'll tell you something about nitro-benzene, and it will put all that one-two-three-four stuff out of your head. Our professor of chemistry, Milligan, always makes a little joke about nitro-benzene to his students, about this time of the year."

"That was going to be my fifth point," said Mike amiably. "Mullen is a graduate of this College and he says Milligan and his nitro-benzene were a byword. He says that Milligan used to recommend the use of nitro-benzene as a poison, because of the four advantages that I named."

"Look at that!" said the Sergeant. "Right under our noses all these years! He should be locked up, so he should."

"That way madness lies, Sergeant," said Daly.

"Still, we'll have to ask Professor Milligan about it," said Mike, "and I would like if you could come with me. He may be difficult——"

"He'll be as pleased as Punch," said Daly. "About the nitro-benzene, that is. But he may be uneasy in another way. You see, Milligan is a kleptomaniac. He has been like that for years." The sergeant moaned and clutched his forehead. "His daughter looks after him, so that he never does any real damage. But you must be careful not to hurt his feelings. He's very sensitive about it."

"So that's the little failing you mentioned last night?" said Mike, who was retaining his calm with some difficulty.

77

"Yes," said Daly. "As you saw, there's no great secret about it, really. But perhaps you can understand better now why Bradley did not want the police in about the place. For all his faults he had a feeling of responsibility towards his staff."

Mike cocked an eye at him.

"You think that that was why?"

Daly looked uncomfortable and then he said suddenly, nodding towards the desk:

"Have you found the anonymous letters?"

"No, but I have found documents which say that Mr. Leahy was going to present this college with fifty thousand pounds. You were here at this house last night when Leahy himself said there must be some good way of spending fifty thousand dollars."

"Now, if it had been the other way around," Daly began with interest.

"I'm thinking," MacCarthy said ingenuously, "that myself and Murphy, here, will have our dinner in the kitchen with the staff, the way we'll have a chance of picking up a bit of information, do you follow——"

"All right, all right," said Mike. "I'm hungry, too."

The sergeant and his silent mate left with great alacrity. Mike conducted Daly out into the hall and locked the study door. Then he went along to the tiny room off the hall where the telephone was, to make arrangements for the post-mortem and the disposal of Bradley.

Standing there waiting for him and trying not to hear the one-sided conversation through the glass-panelled door, Daly suddenly remembered Mrs. Bradley. Mike seemed not to take any interest in her. Daly wondered what she was thinking about, alone in her room with her aspirins, and with the dead body of her obnoxious husband next door. He feared that she might be mourning him from a sense of duty, for he knew that it was largely this sense that had always ruled her life. He glanced at Mike's straight back, which he could see through the glass of the door, observing his long, efficient hand holding the telephone, and the upward lift of his chin that so clearly showed the determination and single-mindedness of his charac-

78

ter. Like a small boy watching a schoolmaster, Daly judged Mike's mood, and he was afraid to slip up the stairs, as he could so easily have done, and visit Mrs. Bradley in her room. Just then Mike turned suddenly and sent a penetrating glance through the glass, as if he knew the direction of Daly's thoughts. It was clear that Mike had some doubt as to whether the old man was able to resist the temptation, for he kept a close watch, through narrowed eyelids, until he put down the telephone.

"Now we can have something to eat," he said blandly, as he came out into the hall. "Then we'll come back and talk to Mrs. Bradley."

8

At the restaurant it seemed as if the entire crowd from the quadrangle had simultaneously felt the need of strength through food. Denny came scurrying over, sibilantly solicitous.

"I'll send you a tray in your rooms, Professor. Don't go in there at all."

He hustled them away from the door. Already their presence had been observed by those who sat near it, and an air of uneasiness had begun to spread through the room.

"It's better this way," said Daly, as he led Mike upstairs. "We are hardly justified in afflicting them all with indigestion."

The first thing that Daly saw, when he came into his study, was the folder containing the notes of his morning lecture. He seized it, like a mother recovering a lost child, and almost covered it with kisses.

"I had forgotten all about it," he said to Mike in an awed tone. "Of course I have the draft at home, but this is absolutely invaluable."

He hugged it to his bosom and looked at Mike over the top with large alarmed eyes. Mike was saved the necessity of replying by the appearance in the doorway of Jennings, whose painful anxiety to please had softened him so that his backbone seemed no longer able to hold him upright.

"I brought up your notes, Professor. I hope you don't mind. I thought you might like to keep them for a kind of souvenir, like——"

"Souvenir your granny!" thundered Daly. "These are a life's work. These are my gift to posterity!"

"Yes, sir," said Jennings piteously. "And I'm bringing up lunch for yourself and Mr. Kenny, in a minute or two."

"Good, good," said Daly with a hard, thoughtful eye on him. "And thanks for minding my notes, Jennings. I should hate to lose them."

When Jennings had gone out Daly said:

"Do you know, that is the first time that Jennings has ever been civil to me. I deduce that he knows something. And I guess what."

"What?" said Mike hopefully.

"Time will tell," said Daly. "I'm doing no prognosticating just now."

In spite of his protests against the idea, Daly talked about nitro-benzene throughout the meal that Jennings presently brought. Mike was amused at this. He knew that, as was usual with him, Daly had translated the crude reality of Bradley's death into terms of imagination, almost of poetry. He no longer saw the physical aspects of it, the sordid violence and the triumph of the powers of darkness. All he saw was that some-one, by poisoning Bradley, had cocked a snook at Daly's mental powers. The prospect of the resultant duel filled him with such an exhilarating excitement that he almost loved both Bradley and his murderer for causing it.

Mike had no objection whatever to discussing murder over his meals. He had long ago become accustomed to this, having eaten with thieves and murderers both before and after their arrest. He induced Daly to tell him Milligan's joke, which was a complicated one about the general suitability of nitro-benzene as a poison. Even those students who failed to see the point always laughed as heartily as Milligan did himself, or as a junior barrister laughs at jokes from the bench.

"Everyone in the College knows the name of nitro-benzene," said Daly, "even those of us who have not the remotest idea of what it is. That was why I exclaimed when you mentioned it, as a Connemara man might if you mentioned the town in America to which all his aunts had emigrated. You will find no clue in that."

"Unless Milligan did it himself," said Mike comfortably, lighting the slim blond cigar that Daly had given him.

"Do kleptomaniacs commit murder?" asked Daly.

81

Mike built up a crazy theory whereby Milligan would have been planning for forty years to murder Bradley, feigning kleptomania and making jokes about nitro-benzene throughout that time, in order to provide himself with protective colouring.

"The snag is that he would have had to see Bradley and take a scunner against him while they were both schoolboys," said Daly. "I should call that an unlikely prospect. Though I seem to remember that he taught Bradley."

"Milligan could have used the same protective colouring even without forty years' premeditation," Mike pointed out. "In our experience, the murderer usually turns out to be the owner of the weapon."

They were disturbed by sounds of a scuffle and the clink of china outside the door. Then it was opened slowly and old Lewis stalked into the room carrying the coffee-tray high as if he bore upon it triumphantly the head of his foe. The fact that he was the merest trifle shaky on his feet only served to make him more majestic.

"The Ignorance of some People," said Lewis. "It makes me blood boil."

He kicked the door shut, with an emphatic backward jerk of his heel. Daly raised an eyebrow sympathetically.

"That Jennings," said Lewis with terrible scorn. "An upstart, sir. A beggar on horseback."

He put down the silver tray at such an angle that Mike had to reach out a long dexterous hand to save the coffee-pot from measuring its length on the table. Lewis turned with extreme care to look at him.

"Never spilled a coffee-pot in me life," he said severely. He swung back to Daly as slowly as a dock crane. "I may say, sir, that Jennings would not behave so badly if he were not encouraged. It's a great mistake to encourage such people. Now, when he brought your luncheon you should have said: 'Where is Lewis?' No more. Just: 'Where is Lewis?'"

"I see that now, Lewis," said Daly apologetically. "I'm afraid I was a trifle upset, on account of the President's death."

"That is no excuse," said Lewis. "As you should know, in

82

the words of the greatest poet in the English language: '*If* you can keep your head when all around are losing theirs——' "

Daly screwed up his face as if he had bitten on a lemon. He stood up and laid a heavy hand on Lewis's shoulder.

"*If* you want to keep your job when all around you are losing theirs, Lewis old boy, you'll go away to your bed, wherever it is, and sleep it off. Here, I'll give you something to make sure that you won't wake up with a headache."

He fished in his pocket, brought out a little tube of tablets and shook out two of them. He clapped them into Lewis's hand and moved him firmly towards the door. Just before he was put outside, Lewis said reproachfully:

"I'm surprised at you, Professor, for having such things so handy in your pockets. But I'll take your advice, because I think you are my friend. Yes, I think you are my friend——"

He pattered off mumbling tearfully to himself. Daly shut the door and came back to drink the cup of coffee that Mike had poured for him.

"Lewis seems to have been down in Biddy Macnamara's celebrating the end of Bradley," he said. "I wouldn't mind paying a call on Biddy myself later on. Lewis couldn't stand Bradley."

Mike raised an eyebrow.

"No, he would not have poisoned him," said Daly. "You see, Lewis can't stand anybody. It's his nature."

"He seems quite attached to you," said Mike.

"Only because I have retired. When I was on the staff it was another story."

"Still, we can't count him out," said Mike. "Who is Biddy Macnamara?"

"She keeps a hostelry called 'The Cow' a few minutes' walk away from the College, out of town. It's quite an old pub. It was out in the open country once, and Biddy still keeps it as it was then, with a big fire and grandmother chairs. The students go there, though they are not supposed to, and all the porters."

"It sounds like a good place to pick up a bit of gossip."

"First rate. And Biddy has a wonderful memory. She knows the name of every bone in the human body, from listening to the chronics droning them out over the fire in the winter evenings." He stopped suddenly. "Of course she could hardly tell you anything useful about this business of Bradley's death."

"You never can tell," said Mike. "We don't like to leave any avenue unexplored."

When they came out into the quadrangle a few minutes later they were just in time to see an ambulance drive away from the President's front door. No one was about except Burren, who was standing on the steps with his hands in his pockets, looking quite unconcerned except for the sardonic twist of his mouth.

"That was Bradley going off," he said, as soon as Mike and Daly were close enough. "They didn't ask me to do the post-mortem. Perhaps you did not know that pathology is my job, Kenny?" He gave a little snorting laugh. "I should like to have seen for myself whether Bradley's heart was black!"

He laughed again, pleased at having shocked them both. Daly recovered himself first.

"You have surpassed yourself, Burren," he said. "You can always be relied upon to leave no stomach unturned."

Burren appeared to acknowledge this as a compliment, for he strolled off looking pleased with himself and obviously savouring his joke for his own amusement. Neither Mike nor Daly made any comment upon him as they waited for Nellie to let them into the house.

"That Professor Burren!" she began at once, while she held the door wide. "I don't care if he was Saint Thomas Aquinas, I'll never let him cross that door again."

"What has he done?" Daly asked innocently.

"Nothing would do him but to come in with the men that were taking the unfortunate President away. Standing behind them cracking jokes and wanting to know who was going to— going to——" She could not bring herself to mention the post-mortem. " 'Twould make a dog strike his father," she finished, "and that's what I told him."

"Good girl," said Daly. "I told him something like the same myself."

84

She looked a little calmer at this. She moved close to them, confidentially, and said in a low voice:

"Do you know, I often tell them at home—they're all a bit touched in this place. 'Tisn't natural to be all the time stuck in books. That Professor Delaney, now, if he was in any other job he'd have been put away long ago. And Professor Milligan would be inside in the body of the jail, so he would. But sure they're too clever, they're not like the rest of us at all."

By the time she had finished this speech, she had talked herself back into a more tolerant attitude. Mike was pleased that she was so articulate, and that she seemed to have an observant eye for the oddities of human behaviour. She would be an invaluable source of information about the events of the day before Bradley's death. He asked her if Mrs. Bradley had yet come downstairs, and learned that she was waiting for him in the drawing-room.

Suddenly Daly found that he did not want to go in with Mike.

"It's not as if I could be of any use to you," he said. "In fact my presence there would make things more difficult, for her and for you. Just tell her that I'll come later on. You don't particularly want me there?"

"Not at all."

Mike was relieved that Daly had volunteered to leave him alone with Mrs. Bradley. He reassured the old man that his presence was not necessary even at the beginning of the interview. Nellie opened the front door again and Daly slipped out with something of the air of a house dog getting away for an illegal, solitary ramble. Watching him thoughtfully Mike could not decide whether Daly was planning to steal a march on him somehow while he was engaged with Mrs. Bradley, or whether he was simply innocently pleased at the postponement of a painful interview with a newly bereaved widow. There was only a moment for such speculations, however, for already Nellie was opening the drawing-room door and announcing his presence in the half-whisper that is commonly used in a house of death.

For all her short dumpiness, to Mike Mrs. Bradley was a

figure of tragedy. It was not that she was in tears, for indeed she seemed to be fully in control of her emotions. He had seen many widows, in the course of his business, and he thought he could recognize the confused and distressed course of her thoughts. The same expression could be seen on the face of the owner of a very old dog who has died—a nagging sense of loyalty born of the habit of living with it, a true conviction that it has never really been loved, relief that it is dead, remorse for former impatience, and a sort of primitive wish to make amends by public mourning. If Mrs. Bradley had been mourning a dog, Mike would not have hesitated to point out to her the advantages of its death. Since it was her husband, it was not so easy to help her.

He began with a few conventional words of sympathy in such a dry tone as not to start any emotional response in her. It was clear that though she was disconcerted for a moment, she accepted the notion that policemen are cool and business-like in the face of murder. She began to answer his questions, hesitantly at first, but gradually becoming more detached and objective, in an effort to match Mike's tone.

She was quite certain that Bradley would not have committed suicide.

"It would never have occurred to him," she said. "No matter how desperate his situation, he would always have believed that there was a special way out for him. If he were on a ship going down in the middle of the Atlantic, he would expect an angel to come from heaven and save him, even if all the other passengers drowned. Do I sound very callous?" she asked suddenly.

"No one can tell us these things but you," said Mike gently. "Please go on."

"He believed in his luck," she said slowly, "and you know, he had good reason. His appointment here, for instance, and the way he became consultant for various mines in Africa, and the way he was invited to give lectures. A great deal of that was luck, as he used to say himself. And he was a terribly *live* person. There seemed to be more of him than of other people. I can't explain what I mean——"

86

"I know," said Mike. "Don't forget that I met him. Did he talk to you about his affairs, his work for the College, disagreements with the staff, anything like that?"

"Hardly ever," she said. "It made things difficult for me sometimes. I used to meet people who expected me to know all about them, and it looked odd when I was quite blank. He didn't know it, but I had learned to tell by his face whether he liked people or not. I used to watch him and plan my own behaviour accordingly, because he didn't like it if I was too friendly with someone with whom he was quarrelling."

Now Mike remembered the anxious eye that she had kept on Bradley during last night's party, as a man working a blast furnace keeps an eye on the thermometer. She told him that Bradley had seemed very content when the guests had gone home. He had poured himself a drink of whiskey—but none for her—and had discoursed to her for ten minutes on the good fortune of the College in having himself as President, since it was he who had ensnared Leahy and his money. He had said that he intended to spend the money on new clubrooms for the students, whether the academic council liked it or no, and that he would present a few pictures at his own expense, to adorn them. Mike gathered that she had been tired and had not listened very deeply. Unintentionally she gave an impression that it was not her habit to listen to Bradley's words, but only to the tone of his voice which told her whether he was in good humour or no. Mike knew that this was a trick of many women who have come to regard their husbands as if they were rather difficult employers. She bore out the truth of his surmise a moment later by saying:

"I think my husband was disturbed about something for the last few weeks. At first I thought it was about the Leahy money, but later I came to the conclusion that there was something else, a more personal thing. He seemed to be in perfect health, but this morning when I—when we—found him, I thought he must have known for some time that he was not well. Then Nellie told me that you were here, and that there was talk of poisoning, and now I don't know what to think."

"If you had known that his life was being threatened

87

would you have understood his behaviour?" Mike asked quickly.

"Was that the explanation?" Her surprise was certainly genuine. "Of course it must have been. It was stupid of me not to have seen it. That is why there was a feeling of resentment in his fear——" She broke off and smiled uncertainly. "You see, I knew him very well."

He asked her about the dinner-party of the evening before, but she could tell him nothing except that Bradley had been anxious that Mr. Leahy should enjoy himself. They had these parties every week or so, Bradley himself making out a list of those who were to be invited. Mrs. Bradley's only business was to provide suitable food and to discourage quarrels among the guests.

"I noticed you do that part very well, last night," said Mike.

"Yes, Burren is rather awful," she said. "But it was hard to blame any of them, really. My husband was a past master of the art of petty persecution, and if he drove someone too far, he had only himself to blame."

Mike was pleased enough at this bitter speech, for it showed that she was beginning to realize that there was no need to deceive him about her feelings. Of course she would have to appear suitably concerned at her husband's death to satisfy the general public, but Mike's work would be greatly lessened by not having to probe through layers of false sentiment and artificial mourning. He asked her if Bradley was at all concerned about money.

"I don't know," she said. "He paid all the household bills and wages. He never gave me any money at all."

"None at all?"

"No." Her tone was quite blank. "I have a little income of my own, less than three hundred pounds a year. I used that for pocket-money, and for clothes, and an occasional little holiday when I felt I needed it. Sometimes I bought clothes in shops where he had an account, just to show him that he could not entirely evade his responsibilities. But I didn't do that very often."

88

"Did he ever give you presents?"

She brightened a little, as if she were unexpectedly amused.

"Not often?" Mike prompted her.

"Sometimes, if there were any publicity to be gained he did give me presents," she said after a pause. "My diamonds, when he was retiring from Africa, my minks when he was made President—but always as if he were making a presentation to an employee with long service. Oh, it's hard to tell, really, what went on in his head. He was a most secretive man. For all I knew, he could have been a millionaire or a pauper."

"Did you never question him about money?"

She gave him such a long look that he thought she was beginning to resent his questions. This time the pause dragged itself out until several minutes had passed. Mike leaned back in his chair, simply waiting for her answer. When it came it did not seem to be the answer to his question.

"My husband had a very highly developed sense of property," she said slowly, as if she were giving a careful résumé of his character. "A thing that belonged to him, even if he did not want it for himself, was not to be handled nor thought about by anyone else. He even hated to see the maids polishing *his* furniture or cleaning *his* shoes, though the fact that they were *his* maids consoled him a little."

Suddenly, as in a picture, Mike got a short, terrifying view of the life of this woman living here in her own peculiar hell, the chattel of her grasping husband. Now, from her words, he began to understand Bradley's attitude about the Leahy money. It was his, that was all. That he had to use a trick to get part of it into his private account he would regard as a tiresome formality. It was clear that he had intended to return some of that part in the form of presents of pictures, for which he would receive great credit and thanks.

Mike felt sure that Leahy's money was the cause of Bradley's downfall. It had been mentioned in the anonymous letters and it had certainly caused a palpable rise in the temperature of last night's dinner-party. Now it seemed that Bradley had already decided on what he intended to do with the money, though his colleagues thought nothing had yet been settled.

Seeing the elementary simplicity of those same colleagues, Mike was quite prepared to find that one of them had poisoned him. A sufficient reason would be that the murderer had different ideas about the disposal of the money, and had discovered that Bradley was going to allow no discussion. He positively blushed at the vision of himself trying to arrest one of the bland, scholarly professors who trotted so purposefully about the College.

Mrs. Bradley looked a little more cheerful now, like a person who has successfully completed an unpleasant task. Though she was old enough to be his mother, she sat there like a child waiting for well-deserved praise, or like a woman to whom no one has spoken a kind word for a great many years. This thought struck him so painfully that he spent the next few minutes in thanking her for her help, assuring her of his consideration, asking after her future plans, advising her to take a holiday and in general showing such concern for her comfort and welfare that he was presently rewarded with floods of tears. Though this distressed him, when she recovered herself she had a determined light in her eye. It was as if she felt that those tears had paid the last of her very nebulous debt to Bradley.

Still, Mike thought as he left her, she had hated her husband enough to have poisoned him. If she had not done so, his consoling words were an act of charity for which he would get a reward in heaven. If she had, then the same words would have the effect of convincing her that she had to deal with a soft-hearted fool, and of making her relax her efforts to cover her guilt.

"Either way, I win," he said to himself with satisfaction as he let himself out into the hall.

9

Hearing faint hoots of laughter from the direction of the kitchen Mike guessed that his two adjutants were pursuing their enquiries there. He went through the old-fashioned baize door from the hall and found himself in a stone-floored corridor. At the far end of it he could see the open door of the kitchen with a red-tiled floor and shining anthracite cooker. On either side of the corridor he found empty wine cellars. A deep laugh rang out again, directing him to the door next to the kitchen. He opened it quickly and stood looking into the room.

It was a pantry, with silver spread out on its wide shelves to be cleaned. Sergeant MacCarthy's long legs seemed to stretch across most of the floor, while he sat back like a sultan in the single chair. Murphy, his aide, leaned against the door-post. The rest of the party consisted of Nellie, with a silver cloth in her hand, and a solid, bright-eyed young woman whom Mike took to be "that Annie" from the kitchen. She and MacCarthy and Murphy had cups of tea in their hands, while Nellie's stood beside her on the shelf.

The sergeant heaved himself upright.

"Just knocked off a few minutes ago for a cup of tea," he said. He waved airily to the two women. "Hop off now, girls. Nellie, you can bring a cup of tea for the Inspector."

They hopped off, as meek as sheep hopping through a gap, taking their tea with them. Mike commended the sergeant gravely for his mastery of them.

"Catch 'em young, treat 'em rough and tell 'em nothing," said MacCarthy. "That's always been my motto."

"Have they told you anything?" Mike asked.

"I was finding out in a general kind of way what visitors the

91

President had yesterday," said the sergeant. He turned suddenly to Murphy, who had stood petrified with embarrassment since Mike's entrance, and said with his habitual lack of tact: "Drink your tea, man, for Pete's sake. The inspector knows you eat and drink sometimes, when there's no one looking." Murphy gurgled unhappily into his teacup. MacCarthy took a large, comfortable swallow from his own and said: "I was thinking that if the doctor is right about the nitro-benzene, Bradley could have had it at the party, or before it, even." He closed one eye, and bent the other, large and round and measuring, upon Mike. "You were at that party yourself, sir, I'm told."

At that moment Nellie brought in a tea-tray and the conversation had to be suspended until she had gone out again. This gave Mike time to assimilate the implications of the sergeant's last remark. Through the facetious suggestion that Mike himself could have murdered the President it was plain to be seen that MacCarthy was hurt at being excluded from his senior's confidence. He had made a similar leading remark earlier. Mike hurried to explain that this was his first opportunity of telling the story of Bradley's appeal to Professor Daly to save his life. He did so now, and added Daly's suggestion that the President could have invented the whole story of the anonymous letters as a façade behind which comfortably and secretly to commit suicide.

"I don't believe in that," said the sergeant. "That's a queer kind of an idea. I knew Bradley well, because this is my district. You can take it from me, he was the sanest man in this College."

"That is what Professor Fox said," Mike remembered.

"But do you know who could have invented it?" MacCarthy held up a dramatic finger. "Professor Daly!"

"Nonsense!"

"Why? We only have his word for it that Bradley told him his life was being threatened."

"But Daly told me that Bradley recognized me and was glad I was here to keep an eye on him. I might have spoken to Bradley about it, and then Daly would have been exposed. Oh, that's all nonsense anyway, because Fox said he saw the letters."

"Um," said MacCarthy regretfully. "All the same, I wouldn't trust that Professor Daly too far. He looks like a man that has something on his mind." He shook his head, his brow black with disfavour. "Him and his jokes. I'd never trust that kind of a man."

Mike rushed to defend Daly, but even while he did so he recalled a very faint discomfort between them which could not have existed between such old friends unless there were a lack of confidence somewhere. The reason for it was probably that Daly distrusted Mike's ability to uncover the murderer without his help.

"Professor Daly visited Bradley yesterday afternoon," said the sergeant insinuatingly, watching him wryly to observe the effect of this suggestion.

"Don't be coy," said Mike pettishly. "I know he did. It was then that Bradley told him he had recognized me. Who else came?"

"Miss Milligan, whose father is a kleptomaniac, according to your Professor Daly. And he manufactures nitro-benzene by the gallon, of course."

Mike ignored this heavy irony, and asked again:

"Anyone else?"

"There was Professor Delaney, who told Nellie that his business concerned rats." The sergeant's voice was expressionless. "And Professors Hamilton and Fox who came together. That's the lot, unless any of these crazy coots came climbing in at the windows."

"Some of those were at the dinner-party afterwards." He told MacCarthy about the little scene concerning the macaroons. "It was Burren who started that. He oozed hatred of Bradley. I wish I knew whether it was then that Bradley was poisoned. Burren could have prepared a poisoned biscuit, I suppose, and when the plate was being returned he could have substituted it for the single biscuit remaining. But he would have had to rehearse the other members of the party to make sure that that would work. The wrong person could so easily

93

have got it. They were quite capable of handing the plate back empty. It would be too uncertain."

"Burren," said MacCarthy thoughtfully. "He's a sour-puss, all right. And the way he talked about the President now that he's dead—'twould turn a horse from his oats. I was there when the ambulance men were taking him away——"

"Yes," said Mike. "Nellie told us. We'll have to find out what is behind all that. What did you learn in the kitchen?"

But all that MacCarthy had learned was that Bradley was as much disliked below stairs as above. A very strong rumour existed in the kitchen that Bradley's methods in acquiring his fortune in Africa were discreditable to him.

"So maybe we'll find that someone had the black on him," said the sergeant comfortably, "and that he done himself in when he was broke."

But Mike did not incline to believe in this theory. He would have expected that Bradley would kill the blackmailer rather than himself, and that he would have done so long before he had exhausted his resources.

"I can't see him committing suicide," said the sergeant after a pause. "He'd always be sure that there was a special trick in the bag for him."

"That is what Mrs. Bradley says, too," said Mike.

"And still," MacCarthy went on in a hurt tone, "he didn't believe in God at all. He explained it all to me one evening that I met him strolling over by the park. Luck, and good fortune, and that class of thing was what he believed in, like a child believing in fairies. Ah, well, he must have got the drop of his life when he died."

While Mike finished his tea they arranged to start enquiries about Bradley's years in Africa, and to include a suggestion that his honesty in general be brought into question.

"That will give them enough to get suspicious on," said MacCarthy. He looked uncomfortable and stammered a word or two. Then suddenly he thundered: "Off with you, Murphy! Are you going to stand there all day?"

Murphy gave a sharp, involuntary yelp. His cup shot off the saucer, but he clutched at it in mid air and saved it from crash-

ing to ruin on the flags. He stood crouched, staring at the
sergeant while his huge hands encircled the china like a hen's
wings. Then he whispered:

"Yes, sir."

He laid down the cup and saucer and got out of the room as
if it had been a cage of lions. In the following silence they heard
him move up the corridor as slowly as a sleepwalker.

"What are you doing to poor Murphy?" said Mike in
astonishment, when the sound had died away.

"I didn't want him to hear what I'm going to say to you,"
said MacCarthy, looking a little shamefaced. "Anyway, how
was I to know he's so sensitive?"

Mike made no reply to this. He had almost bitten his
tongue at the sergeant's shout, but he had no intention of
admitting it. MacCarthy went on, heavily explanatory:

"It's not that I would ever be slow to do my duty, sir. You
know I fought three gunmen that were trying to raid the safe
in Walsh's shop last year, and kept them off until help arrived.
It's not that I'm afraid. But don't ask me to go questioning
those professors. I could never stand it. It's the way they look
at you, kind of slow, and grinning at something inside in their
own heads all the time. You can't hurry them and you can't
frighten them. They know too much about everything. And
they wouldn't mind a bit going to gaol, even. Professor
Badger, now, he says he'd like gaol. Quiet and peaceful, and
plenty of time for reading and writing, no children around the
place, lots of sleep, plain wholesome food, interesting company
—that's what he told me a few weeks back."

"Never mind, Sergeant," said Mike soothingly. "I'll talk to
the professors myself, if you'll handle Nellie and Jennings and
Lewis and the rest of the porters. There is a cook here, I'm
told, as well as 'that Annie'."

"I'll talk to them with the greatest of pleasure," said Mac-
Carthy, "if you'll do the professors. Mind you, I like them well
enough, and I know nearly all of them on account of living
so near the College. But I come all over queer when I think of
asking them where they spent yesterday and would they have
any reason for polishing off the President." He looked at

Mike with deep respect. "You have a great nerve, sir, so you have."

Mike could not bring himself to demolish his own reputation at a single blow by confessing that he, too, was frightened of the task before him.

It was in a depressed mood that he left the sergeant, who was on his way to the kitchen, and let himself out of the President's Lodging again. Mrs. Bradley was not about when he hurried through the hall, and he was glad of this, for he had not asked her permission to go through to the service part of the house.

When he came out into the quadrangle he found that the afternoon had slipped away and a gilded gloom had fallen on the buildings. He walked over towards the main door, from which a wide river of light flowed out on to the gravel. The moment that he stepped into its radiance, Jennings came darting out on to the steps, the picture of obsequious goodwill.

"I was watching out for you, sir. The President asked me to bring you over to him at once."

"The President? What are you talking about?" Mike stopped dead in his astonishment.

Jennings laughed in a high whinny.

"I should have said the *acting* President," he said. He rubbed his hands together in an ingratiating gesture that Mike found rather pathetic. "The Governors met and appointed Professor Daly acting President. A great honour for him, but he's worthy of it. Yes, he's worthy of it."

And Jennings had picked up an inkling of it in advance, said Mike to himself grimly. He studied him while he followed him towards the President's office. Jennings was the sort of subject that monarchs dream about. The king to him was always splendid, noble, praiseworthy, to be defended with his very life. A new king or an old king—it was all the same to him. In fact, the passing of one king and the crowning of the next only served to stimulate him to further transports of fealty. He saw only the crown, never the face underneath it.

At a heavy, carved oak door, pillared and panelled impressively, he paused for a reverent moment. Then he swung the door silently inwards and said in a voice almost choked with respect:

"Inspector Kenny, President."

Mike was shocked to find that he had contracted some of Jennings's awe. He felt his heart pound as he moved silently into the room. The door clicked shut behind him. The little sound awoke him as if from a trance, and he saw Daly, adorned with a devilish grin, sitting at a massive desk watching him.

"You haven't changed a bit," said Mike indignantly. "I thought from Jennings's behaviour that you would be robed like Finn MacCool, and at least six inches taller than when I saw you last."

Daly wagged his head appreciatively.

"Do you know, Mike, I feel the lust for power rising up in me. It's Jennings that has done it. I feel an almost uncontrollable longing to make him lie down on the floor so that I can put my foot on his neck. Isn't that a terrible thing?"

"Terrible," said Mike solemnly. "How did it happen?"

"It was because I succeeded in dispersing the students this morning when Foxy failed," said Daly. "They had a meeting and nominated me as acting President, if I would be good enough to undertake the job. I was good enough, because I have always had a secret longing to sit in this chair." He thumped the arms of it appreciatively. "They had several reasons for choosing me. The main one is that being seventy-four years old I can stake no claim to succeed Bradley. Anyway, here I am, lord of the fowl and the brute. Plenty of fowls and brutes about," he finished meditatively.

Mike was whole-heartedly pleased with Daly's appointment, not only for the child-like pleasure that it afforded his friend, but also for the help and understanding of which he would now be certain. In the huge, timeless air of the College, for the first time in his life he had begun to doubt the importance of his profession. Bradley seemed already almost forgotten. No one mourned him. The formalities of his disposal were carried out and a successor appointed with a monastic detachment that Mike found devastating to his notions of life and death. The problem of the cause of his death seemed to arouse interest still, but only in the same way as would the problem of discovering the author of a medieval manuscript. As if he had been following Mike's thoughts, Daly said:

"You won't find the staff very anxious to talk about Bradley from what I can gather. They are like children whose cross nurse has been given the sack. They'll forget him quite soon."

"I'll have to try to persuade them to talk," said Mike. "I'm relying on you to help me."

Daly smiled with simple delight, but before he had time to reply Jennings came creeping in at the door with a salver on which lay an envelope. He slithered over to the desk and held the salver under Daly's nose. Within ten seconds of Daly's taking the letter in his hand, Jennings was out through the door again like an eel. Daly looked after him with raised eyebrows.

"Fellow is like a caricature of himself," he said. He glanced at the envelope and then handed it to Mike. "This is for you. Jennings seems to think I should censor your correspondence."

He watched anxiously while Mike opened the envelope and in the little pause that followed he seemed to have difficulty in restraining himself from demanding to know the contents.

"It was nitro-benzene, all right," said Mike softly. "Good man, Mullen. Now at last we know where to begin."

"Milligan?"

"Milligan first," said Mike. "I hope he has not gone home. We didn't try to make everyone stay in the College. There are too many of them."

"Milligan hardly ever goes home," said Daly briskly. "Come along and I'll show you where to find him."

10

Professor Milligan's department was housed in a long, one-storied red-brick building a short distance away from the main buildings. They were silent as they walked towards it through the gathering darkness.

Mike felt that Daly was longing to implore him not to mention Milligan's little failing, but that he was afraid to do so lest he cast too much emphasis upon it. They paused at the foot of a shallow flight of stone steps that led up to the door. To the right they could see through long windows into a lighted laboratory. Milligan was there, tall and thin and slightly stooped, moving up and down before a bench on which he had erected some extremely impressive apparatus. He prodded at it with the concentrated incisiveness of a heron fishing off a mudbank. He had the ageless dignity of a heron, too, in his narrow grey suit and black smoking cap, which would have looked bizarre on a lesser man. His expression was mild and scholarly, and he smiled gently to himself as if he found life pleasant.

The door was open and Daly led the way through the hall to the laboratory. Milligan looked up with a welcoming smile.

"Ah, come along in, Daly. Badger was here just now to tell me about you. How does it feel?"

"Much the same," said Daly airily, "you know, as friend Burns would say: 'Rank is but a ten-guinea pants. A tail's a tail, for a' that.'"

Milligan chuckled with delight.

"Badger tells me that Burren is very sore about it. It seems he thought he was the obvious choice." He looked at Mike with mildly interested light blue eyes. "You are Inspector Kenny, I think? Didn't we meet at the President's Lodging this afternoon?" He shook Mike's hand with solemn care. Then his face lit up with a smile that was both guilty and smug as he said: "Badger told me, too, that Bradley was poisoned with nitro-benzene."

"How under heaven did Badger find that out?" said Mike angrily.

Milligan said:

"Then it's true. Ha! Who would have thought it, after all these years." He nodded to himself. "I have always said it was a first-rate poison."

He might have been talking about an unsuspected Old Master whose worth had at last been discovered.

"Inspector Kenny wants to know if you could suggest where the nitro-benzene could have come from," said Daly with no great delicacy.

"From here, most likely," said Milligan, staring. "My students make it every year. A child could make it."

"A child who knew how," said Mike.

"Every child knows how," said Milligan with a shrug. "I shouldn't think there would be any difficulty in getting it. Bradley himself would have known how to make it. He had a science degree as well as a degree in engineering."

"Had he been over here lately?" Mike asked eagerly, for he had not lost all hope of discovering that Bradley had taken his own life.

"He was always nosing about," said Milligan, with a little snort. "I ordered him off in the end. Ha! I did, indeed. Fellow put his hand on a most delicate piece of apparatus and shoved it all out of line. Said he was looking at it. 'Be off with you,' I said to him. 'If you were not the President I'd box your ears for that!' Ha! He went away, all right. Great clumsy oaf!"

He frowned like an angry monkey. He looked capable of murder just then. And, thought Mike in despair, he would need stronger motive than that Bradley had dislocated his apparatus. One of Mike's customers had been an old maid who had murdered her neighbour for stepping on the cat.

"How long have you known Bradley?" he asked.

"He's a little younger than I am," said Milligan. "Seven or

eight years. I was an assistant in this department when he was a student."

"Then you taught him?"

"I tried," said Milligan. "Heaven knows I tried. He was one of those people who seem to know everything that's required of them, and still somehow manage to remain ignorant. He was always self-satisfied, even when he was a boy. That put up a barrier between him and the knowledge that he was pursuing. I told him that. Oh, yes, I told him. It was when he was being conferred with his B.Sc. 'You may have got first-class honours, Bradley,' I said to him, 'but you know no more chemistry than the sole of my boot.' No flair, you see, no flair. He was quite annoyed with me, I remember that. I explained to him that the reason he was no good was that he had a selfish nature which would not allow him to become absorbed in his subject. I advised him to go into industry, and make money. I said that that was the only course open to chaps like him. No, he didn't like that."

Milligan was beginning to look happier now, as he recalled these ancient, inspired words. Not for the first time Mike felt a pang of pity for Bradley.

"I warned them when he was being appointed to Mineralogy," Milligan went on, "but cows in Connacht have long horns and they insisted on having him. Besides, I think Africa is not the best place for learning a social sense. My daughter Sodia tells me he treated the students as if they were black."

"Had you not seen Bradley between the time when he got his degree and his return as professor of mineralogy?" Mike asked.

"No," said Milligan. "He did come home for holidays, but I did not see him then. I had no interest in his type, you see. They upset the other students."

And that, to Milligan, was obviously a great crime. Suddenly he looked directly at Mike and said:

"I'd be much obliged if you would arrest a student called Tennyson-Smith and take him away. He has been, as he says, having a shot at first Arts for three years now, with no success, and still he feels free to take out my daughter Sodia, who gets first class honours every time."

"Has Tennyson-Smith any connection with Bradley?" Mike asked.

Milligan looked disappointed for a moment and then he gave a little jerk of pleasure as he said:

"He was at dinner at Bradley's on the night before he died. Bradley actually asked him and Sodia to dinner together, though he knew how I hate that association."

Mike explained gently that this would make a tenuous reason, especially as Tennyson-Smith was not a sufficiently skilled person to make nitro-benzene successfully.

"I would have made it for him if he had said what he wanted it for," said Milligan magnanimously.

Since it had become obvious that Milligan was not taking him seriously, the policeman in Mike had been wrestling with the humanitarian. Now, quite suddenly, the policeman won. Seeing Mike's expression change Daly gave a little squeak of dismay, but Mike was already saying:

"Did Bradley ever threaten to retire you because of your habit of picking up things that do not belong to you? Judging by Bradley's character as you have revealed it, I can't see how he could have restrained himself."

Milligan groped for a tall stool that stood by the bench and leaned against it. The mischievous light went out of his eyes, and a look of unutterable pain took its place. Daly felt a sudden urgent desire to stab his friend Inspector Kenny to the heart. Mike was watching Milligan with the intense, unblinking eye of a fisherman who feels a bite. Daly felt a little flicker of physical terror go through him as he realized how completely he had lost control of the situation. But there was nothing whatever that he could do, except to tell himself feverishly and hopelessly that any other policeman w uld have been far less considerate.

Milligan's face was grey and he seemed to have difficulty in moving his lips. He twitched his head sideways, like a frightened robin, and then he seemed to draw himself in with a long, terrible effort. When he spoke his voice was carefully controlled.

"Yes, Bradley did that."

"When?"

"Last week."

There was a pause. A little voice inside Mike said: "Aha!" Aloud he said gently with the kindness that he would show to a condemned man:

"Tell me about it."

With a quick movement Professor Daly started for the door. Milligan looked up and said mildly:

"Are you leaving me, too, John? Then I am lost."

"I thought you would like me to go away," said Daly, but he turned back instantly and settled himself against the bench beside Milligan.

Mike said again:

"Tell me about your conversation with Bradley."

"It was the morning after I had ordered him out of the lab," said Milligan. He brightened a little at the recollection of this victory. "That fellow, Jennings, came over here, and told me that the President wanted to see me. I sent him back to say that I was busy, but that I would try to see him in the afternoon. That annoyed Bradley because he had a strange notion that we were his minions, to be summoned at his pleasure. I had two further messages before luncheon. When I saw Jennings approaching for the fourth time I locked the outer door of the lab. When I did go to see Bradley, at about five in the afternoon, he was in a great taking. What he had wanted me about was something trivial, that could easily have been settled over the telephone. He was in such a fury that he almost forgot to tell me about it."

Then Milligan went dumb at the recollection of this scene, and it took great patience and skill on Mike's part before he could draw from him the end of the story. Since Milligan had passed his sixty-fifth birthday he could only be continued from year to year at the President's pleasure. It had become obvious to Milligan quite early that Bradley had no intention of retiring him. Milligan was an ornament to the College and his removal would have raised a storm of protest. But Bradley had wanted to tease him in revenge for the insult that he had suffered at Milligan's hands the day before, and to show Milligan that he

103

had him in his power. Milligan had understood all this and Bradley knew that he did. Still Bradley had kept the terrible game going for about half an hour. At the end of that time Milligan had been in a state of collapse. Now in his distress his words were jerky but meticulously chosen.

"I thought of murder when I left him," he said. "I thought of that. Not nitro-benzene. Too pleasant. You go into an abrupt coma. Never wake up. All those nasty things like the blood turning black and so on—that all happens while the victim is unconscious. I thought of hatchets. Ropes. Cliffs. Big, heavy things—to hit him on the head with. But I didn't do any of them. No. I couldn't."

"Why not?" asked Daly gently.

Milligan turned to him forcefully.

"I'd have had to go near him. Close to him. I couldn't do that. He had a nasty aura of some kind. Did you ever feel it? It prickled you. Gave you a headache. Did you ever feel it?"

"A little," said Daly.

"You were lucky." He reached for a clean beaker off a shelf, ran some water into it from the tall, curved tap on the bench sink and drank the water with slow deliberation. Then he turned back to Mike, his manner quite changed. "Please forgive this exhibition, Mr. Kenny. You started it yourself, you know, by accusing me of murder." A slightly quizzical look came into his eye as Mike began to protest. "Oh, I don't mind. I might have done it, if I had had the courage, or if I could have stood near him for long enough. I never thought of poison. I'm a hopeless shot, by the way. But now I'm rather glad that I didn't, because of Sodia. She would have hated it. I don't show her much consideration, poor child, but that would have been the last straw. I didn't mean to tell anyone about this, and I was sure that Bradley would not. I hope you won't have to broadcast it?"

"Of course not," said Mike.

He added an uncomfortable apology which Milligan waved away, saying:

"I'm glad I told you. It clears the air. Now you will know why I sing about my work." He picked up a flask which stood on the bench and swung it expertly until the colourless liquid it contained swirled about. Then he held it up to the light and said:

"Tch, tch!"

Daly pulled at Mike's sleeve and they moved towards the door. Milligan waved vaguely with his free hand and began to sing falsetto, very quietly:

> *When I am dead, my dearest, sing no sad songs for me.*
> *Plant thou no roses at my head, nor shady cypress tree.*

Outside, in the hallway, Mike leaned weakly against the wall and said:

"What goes on in that man's head?"

"A great variety of things," said Daly, "as you heard. He tells the truth because he is a good chemist."

"But not all of it," said Mike. "He did not deny that Bradley had accused him of stealing things from the College, but he did not tell us which things Bradley mentioned."

"Do you think that was important?"

"It could be. I'll have to ask his daughter."

"I suppose so," Daly sighed.

"And I'll have to see Burren. How did he know that Bradley's heart was black? That's not such a joke now that we hear it really was turned black by the action of the poison."

Outside on the steps they looked in at Milligan again. He was working at his experiment now with renewed energy, wrinkling his nose like a conscientious rabbit, as he bent over the bench.

"He hasn't quite cleared the air yet," said Mike softly. "The reason why I'm not bringing him away by the scruff of the neck is that he sounded so surprised and pleased that nitrobenzene was the poison used. And his rage at the memory of Bradley's threats to retire him—that was all wrong, too. He should have been forgiving, even patronizing towards Bradley if he had killed him for that."

"Milligan is no actor," said Daly, as they walked back to the quadrangle. "When he has something to conceal he becomes surly and uncivil. One can tell at once that he has been up to something. After having met him in that humour most of his acquaintances would go straight home and count the spoons. I'm very fond of Milligan," he added after a moment. "I wonder if he is more odd than Delaney, or Burren, or Badger?"

"In my business," said Mike, "you learn that what we call normality is never more than skin-deep. The reason why these people seem so odd may be that they have never found it necessary to lay on a veneer of respectability."

"And if they had laid it on," said Daly, "your first business would be to dig it off again. So you really have nothing to complain about."

11

"Dinner," said Daly, when they reached the quadrangle. "When life looks black that is the answer. It restoreth my soul. I'll give you five minutes to wash your hands."

Presently on their way to the restaurant they were joined by Hamilton. Daly was instantly cheered by the sight of his round, innocent face.

"I'll have dinner with you, if I may," said Hamilton. "What have you been doing to my future father-in-law?"

Daly stopped dead, so that Fox who had been hurrying to catch up on them, almost cannoned into him.

"Who is your future father-in-law?" Daly asked, covering his eagerness with a kind of desperate calm that amused Mike, though he did not dare to show it.

"Milligan, of course," said Hamilton, with a fat chuckle. "I'm going to marry Sodia."

"When?" Daly demanded.

"Oh, time will tell that," said Hamilton. "She doesn't know about it yet. She's a young thing and cannot leave her mother."

"I thought her mother was dead," said Mike obtusely, and received a pitying glance from Daly.

"I must dispose of this Tennyson-Smith wart-hog first," Hamilton explained. "We couldn't allow a fine girl like Sodia to be wasted on him. She's a wonderful person, Daly, believe me, and she has an uncanny insight into bio-chemistry."

He said this in the reverent tone that another man would use to describe the physical beauties of his beloved, and he followed it with the traditional and genuine lover's sigh of admiration.

"Who told you that we were talking to Milligan?" Mike asked.

Hamilton looked at him as if he were a backward child and said:

"We don't have to be told those things. We just know. Of course we may have been watching to see would you start with Milligan," he conceded, "seeing that Bradley was poisoned with nitro-benzene, and in view of the fact that Bradley was threatening only last week to retire Milligan—Mr. Kenny, what can the matter be?"

Mike's sharp yelp of dismay had brought them all to a halt outside the dining-room door. Now he stood looking Hamilton up and down, breathing hard in his exasperation. Hamilton returned the look with wide-open child-like eyes. Then he said:

"Have I done something wrong?"

"I'd like to have a talk with you afterwards," said Mike meaningly.

"Don't look at me like that," Hamilton pleaded. "I can't help seeing a hole through a ladder, can I? I shouldn't have mentioned Milligan at all, only for Sodia."

"Oh, dear, I hope it wasn't Milligan that did it," Fox was muttering half to himself. "He's such a dear, good fellow. I don't know what we should do. And there's Badger, I meant to tell you, Mr. Kenny. I found him in the President's office just now going through the filing-cabinet. That sort of thing looks very bad. I told him so. I did indeed."

"Did he say what he wanted?" asked Mike.

"He said he was looking for a letter he wrote to Bradley once. He thought it might be there on some file and he didn't want anyone to find it and read it. I got on quite well with Bradley myself, but I must admit that he brought out the worst in people. What do you think, Daly, while you are in office, would it not be well to have a sort of general amnesty? You could easily destroy all those letters of a personal nature and say nothing about it."

"A very good idea," said Daly. "We'll talk about it again."

As Fox showed no sign of moving away, Daly asked him to join them at dinner. He was pleased that he had done so when he saw how eagerly Fox accepted the invitation.

108

"You know, I'm rather low-spirited this evening," he said as if this were something that should cause surprise. "I was closely associated with Bradley, and I think I knew him better than any of you did. His private character was a great deal better than his public one." Mike remembered Mrs. Bradley and smiled wryly at this. "It's a terrible thing to think that if he had had more control over himself he would be alive and with us this evening."

"Terrible," said Hamilton sardonically.

"Then you think he was poisoned by someone whom he had injured?" Mike asked.

"I don't know," said Fox. "I can't imagine what else could have happened. Everyone seems to have hated him. Look at that disgraceful thing they did to him last night, at his own dinner-table." He rubbed his forehead as if to stimulate his brain from without. "I can't think clearly to-day. I never have trouble with the students, but to-day I just couldn't do anything with them. I heard myself twittering at them like an old woman, and still I could not do any better."

"That's because you haven't been eating sweets," said Hamilton. "Sweets are a great stimulant. Still I'm glad you've taken my advice about them."

Fox glared, but Hamilton was impassively drinking his soup.

"Never mind, Foxy," said Daly kindly. "Eat up your soup and you'll find that things will improve."

Fox did so and presently looked a little less worried. The rest of the company in the dining-room was not in the least depressed at Bradley's end. Indeed, it seemed to have stimulated them to an unaccustomed friendliness with each other. Professors who would normally have allowed their colleagues to expire for lack of salt now passed it assiduously up and down the tables with polite ejaculations. Still they kept their eyes fixed on Daly's table and their ears cocked to hear as much of the conversation as possible. The students' eyes darted from the professors' tables to Daly's. Even under cover of their chatter Mike did not feel free to join in the conversation. His companions took no notice whatever of this restraint, for they were too busy with their own speculations.

"I met Mr. Leahy going about like a tigress bereft of her young," said Hamilton, happily falling upon a fillet steak with *maître d'hôtel* butter. "I wonder what will happen about his money now. What would you say, Foxy?"

Fox looked distinctly affronted at this form of address from so young a man. Hamilton, masticating his steak with enjoyment, took no notice of this but waited with interest for his reply.

"I haven't asked Mr. Leahy," said Fox after a moment, "but I assume that he will go ahead as if Bradley were still with us."

"I shouldn't bank on that, if I were you," said Hamilton. "Mr. Leahy spent most of yesterday with Bradley. Now he feels cheated, I think, as if someone had run over his dog."

"How do you know what he feels?" said Fox testily.

"He told me," said Hamilton calmly.

Watching his pleasure in the sensation he had caused, it occurred to Mike that Daly forty years ago must have been very like Hamilton now.

"I've seen rather a lot of Mr. Leahy," said Hamilton. "He took a fancy to me because I have just come back from America. He gets lonesome sometimes, he says, lonesome and uneasy." He reproduced Leahy's twang without effort. "He says he's going right back to the U.S. without any more delay, yes, sir, he is."

"When?" said Fox curtly.

"Three or four days," said Hamilton. "He says he has a few things to clear up or he would be gone before the end of the week."

"I must see him." Fox looked as if he would burst into tears. "He can't slip out now. He's gone too far for that." He drew a long sobbing breath and let it out slowly and with a kind of grating restraint as he said: "This is the last straw. Whoever is responsible for Bradley's death has a lot to answer for. Not only does he deprive our College of the most energetic President it has ever had, but of a benefactor who would have——"

"Don't beef, Foxy," said Daly gently.

Fox glanced quickly around at the grinning students and lowered his voice to say:

"Sorry. I'm upset. I shouldn't be here at all, really. I'm not fit to have a meal in public to-day."

He made as if to leave the table but Daly restrained him by saying that his departure after that outburst would cause unpleasant comment and that they would all leave soon. He prevailed upon him to drink a glass of wine and presently Fox seemed to regain control of himself again, though he looked as glum as a funeral. Hamilton appeared rather disappointed, as if he had been hoping for some entertainment from Fox, but Daly was quite obviously relieved.

On a signal from Mike, Daly said that they would not take coffee this evening. They passed out of the restaurant in a body. As soon as they were outside the door Mike said firmly:

"Good night, Professor Fox, Professor Hamilton. I hope I shall see you both in the morning."

Then he put his hand firmly under Daly's elbow and marched him away towards the stairs. Hamilton uttered a mild squeak, but recovered himself when Fox said a mechanical:

"Good night."

"Good night," said Hamilton also, and he sounded amused.

In Daly's room they paused only for long enough to take their overcoats, for Daly said that Milligan's house was ten minutes' walk away. As they walked down the dark avenue, Daly said, with a sidelong glance at Mike:

"Still after Milligan?"

"And Miss Milligan," said Mike without expression.

"Sodia? How can you possibly——?"

"She doesn't exactly behave like a normal young girl," said Mike. "She could make nitro-benzene—I think someone said she has some knowledge of chemistry?"

"No one said it," said Daly sharply. "But she has. Hamilton mentioned bio-chemistry. Sodia is a medical student. But why should a student poison Bradley?"

"This student may have had good reason," said Mike. "She was accustomed to protecting her father—an unnatural responsibility for a young woman in any event. Quite obviously she has more than her share of mother-instinct or she would never stomach that Tennyson-Smith."

"What a strange line of evidence for a Peeler to follow," said Daly.

"Wasn't it from yourself I learned it?" Mike retorted. "Psychology, and motives, and seeing into people's minds. It's a very good line with people like these, and I'm most thankful to you for teaching it to me. Miss Milligan behaved last night like a murderer. To-day, she cleared off home after your lecture and has not been seen since."

"How do murderers behave?" asked Daly hotly. "She behaved like a girl who has something on her mind, I'll admit, but you have no reason whatever for concluding that it was murder——"

He waited with pathetic eagerness for Mike to give reasons for his statement, but Mike would say nothing. It was not until they reached Milligan's house that he spoke again:

"Don't give away any information, if you please. This is to look like a routine enquiry."

"She'll never believe that," said Daly. "Sodia has more brains in her little finger——"

"Now, don't finish that sentence," said Mike. He was seized with a momentary compassion for Daly. "And don't come in, if you don't want to. I have Sergeant MacCarthy waiting inside."

"Then you're really going to arrest her?" Daly's voice was thin with shock.

"No, not necessarily. We don't know. Dammit, man, how can we know? I think you should go back to the College. I'll call in there on my way home."

"No, thank you. I'll come in with you. And I promise to behave."

Milligan's house was old red brick, faced with granite. In the pillars at either side of the front door specks of mica glittered in the light of the street lamp on the pavement. A bulky shadow moved behind the blind. An elderly woman in a white coat opened the door to Mike's knock. Daly had walked behind Mike across the little gravel sweep and up the shallow flight of steps, as if to accentuate his determination to play a subordinate role. But he was incapable of keeping this up for long. Now he stepped forward before Mike had time to speak and said:

"Mr. Kenny and I would like to see Miss Milligan, Mary."

"She's inside in the drawing-room," said Mary, "and there's a colossal big man within with her. I'll tell her you're here."

She glanced curiously at Mike but made no comment. They waited in the hall while she went into the drawing-room. Mike looked around him with interest. It was a fine old house, but the paintwork was chipped and the dark red flowered wall-paper looked as if it dated from the days of Queen Anne. The glass over the marble chimney-piece was so spotted with age that when Mike looked at himself in it, a grey ghost looked back at him.

The drawing-room, when they were brought into it a moment later, was much better. There was a good fire, and clean old covers on the chairs and sofa, faded almost white. There were open shelves of books everywhere. The carpet was Persian, made to last for a century.

While Mary closed the door behind them, Mike said:

"I hope I haven't delayed you too long, Miss Milligan. I couldn't have come earlier."

"It's all right," said Sodia carelessly. "The sergeant has been entertaining me with funny stories."

The sergeant blushed crimson. Mike stared at him, fascinated. Daly said sharply:

"Stop that, Sodia!"

He went across and closed the curtains. They were black, with a marvellously haphazard Chinese design of flowering trees and birds, in white.

"Professor Badger was here just now," said Sodia, who had not moved from her chair beside the fire. "He told me that you had been to interview my father in his lab."

"That is so," said Mike quietly, concealing with an effort his annoyance. "Professor Badger will also have told you the reason."

"He says that the President was poisoned with nitro-benzene, and that you are convinced that my father did it." Suddenly her voice was sharp. "If you have already arrested him,

113

please tell me at once. Above all things, I hate having bad news broken gently."

Her hands became claws and she seemed to brace herself to receive a shock. Mike crossed deliberately to the other side of the fire. MacCarthy's loud breathing in the silence reminded him of cows in a country lane at night. Then Daly sat down on the edge of the sofa, rather suddenly. Mike said:

"No, we have not arrested your father. Why should we?"

"Badger said—and now Professor Daly came with you—it looked as if——"

"Badger is an old gossip," said Mike.

"He said you know about my father's habit of—taking away things," she said. "Badger said that made you suspect my father of murder. Badger said that you think my father killed Bradley because of that silly trick that Bradley played on him last week."

"Just wait until I see Badger," said Daly between gritted teeth. "Just wait."

"Badger said I was not to worry about the future," said Sodia. "I could go and stay with himself and Mrs. Badger while my father was on trial."

"A fate worse than death," murmured Daly. "What did you say?"

"I thanked him," said Sodia, "like a perfect lady."

Though she was reassured by Mike's attitude, it was clear that she had been very much frightened. The reaction left her on the verge of hysteria, which showed momentarily in the flash of her green eyes. Mike said casually:

"You make no great secret of the fact that Professor Milligan is a kleptomaniac."

"No. It's much better not to. I don't broadcast it, of course. He wouldn't like that."

"Then you did not take the President's threats seriously?"

"No. Neither did my father."

"But it worried him, just the same?"

"No. I said no. He and the President understood each other. My father took no notice whatever."

"I see." Mike achieved a disappointed sigh. "In that case,

neither of you would have had any reason for wishing Bradley dead."

"Neither of us! You're not thinking of me? I was quite friendly with the President. Why, I had dinner with him on the night before he died. You were there yourself, don't you remember?"

"I remember." Mike watched her while she protested and observed that she was watching him just as closely. He said carefully: "We think it possible that he was poisoned at that dinner?"

She started to say:

"Nonsense!"

Then suddenly she closed her mouth tight and covered it with her hand, as if to ensure that no further words would emerge from it. Mike spoke slowly and carefully.

"The people at that dinner were not especially friendly to Bradley, as you have just realized. You seem to find it very shocking that I should consider you as a possible poisoner. I'll tell you why I do, and then you can demolish all my reasons. MacCarthy, old man, please don't snort," he finished mildly.

"I'm going out into the hall," said MacCarthy shortly.

"No offence?"

"No, sir," said MacCarthy, without expression.

There was a pause while he went out of the room. Then Mike cocked an eye at Sodia and said:

"That's better, I think?" She nodded impatiently, and Mike went on: "When your father becomes excited his—little failing —becomes more pronounced. Professor Daly told me that a short while ago, in defence of your father. I, myself, saw him put ashtrays in his pockets in the President's study this morning. He was excited then about Bradley's death. Everyone was. I'm not using that in evidence against him. But I suggest that after Bradley had threatened to retire him Professor Milligan was furiously angry. I suggest that in his excitement he took something valuable, something that perhaps could not be returned. I can imagine how it would seem that the only solution was to poison Bradley before he could find out about it. You assured me a moment ago that your father took Bradley's threats in good part. From my own observation I must disagree with you there. When I spoke to your father a little while ago about that interview with Bradley, the very recollection of it made him speechless with rage."

She started up, but Daly said:

"I think he's all right. He was singing when we left him."

She sank back into the armchair again. Mike went on quickly:

"I have no doubt but that I could find out whether there is any truth in my theory, if I made enquiries in other places. But I never begin that way. I always find that it gives less pain to everyone if I go directly to the people concerned. It often saves time, too." He made a little gesture with his hands. "Of course this method doesn't always work."

"I think it will work this time," she said quietly, after a pause.

"I haven't really been very secretive about it. I would have liked not to have it all come out, but it's not worth while telling any more lies about it."

Neither Mike nor Daly moved. Daly noticed that for all her blasé air, she was still young enough to have hoped that she had shocked them. Presently she went on:

"My father took a gold chalice out of Delaney's museum. It was immediately after he had been with Bradley. He had gone up to the museum to find Delaney. I suppose he wanted someone to talk to. Delaney wasn't there. The chalice was in the little room—it's more like a cupboard, really—off the museum. Delaney had brought it in there to clean it, or make a drawing of it or something. My father would never have opened a glass case and taken it out, but when he looked in the little room to see if Delaney was there, he saw the chalice on the table. He just put it in his pocket. The top of it stuck right out. Only the foot fitted into his pocket. It happened that no one saw him on the way home. If Delaney had met him he would have just taken the chalice back."

"When did you find out about it?" Mike asked.

"Not until next morning. It was lying on his dressing-table."

"Lying?"

"Yes. The foot was broken off it."

"What did you do?"

"I didn't recognize it at first. I wrapped it up in tissue paper and put it away. I asked my father about it during the morning. He told me where it had come from. He always tells me at once. I couldn't put it back broken, so I sent it to be mended."

"Where did you send it?"

"I got a friend of mine to take it to a jeweller." She named a large Grafton Street shop. Mike asked patiently:

"What is your friend's name?"

"Tennyson-Smith. James. Not Jim."

"I'll remember not to call him Jim," said Mike. "But Bradley found out about it before you were able to get it back?"

"Yes. The shop sent him a bill for eight pounds. Rather steep, I thought. But the President didn't seem to mind that. He sent for me yesterday afternoon and was very nice about it all and insisted on giving me two five-pound notes to pay for the repairs. It was James's fault, of course, for telling the jewellers that the chalice belonged to the College. It was then that the President asked us both to come to dinner last night. I didn't want to, but he seemed very anxious that we should. After his kindness about the money—and everything—I thought it would be rude to refuse. I had a terrible time persuading James to come. He thought I should go alone. James", Sodia explained carefully, "is not very bright."

Daly felt his heart leap at this comment. Mike was still asking questions.

"Did your father say how the chalice had got broken?"

"He said it just broke while he was taking it out of his pocket. It was very old—it belonged to Saint Malachy or someone."

"Where did the President get the money that he gave you to pay for the chalice?"

"Out of his wallet, of course. Where else?"

"Where, indeed?" Mike stood up. "I'm glad you told me all about it, Miss Milligan. Is your father a great friend of Professor Delaney?"

"He's very fond of Delaney. They have a great deal in common. They often dine together and Delaney comes down to the lab, sometimes for tea out of a beaker."

"Did Professor Delaney miss the chalice?"

"He had just missed it when I went to tell him about it that morning. He was very worried at first, because he was afraid that the President would say he had been careless in leaving it about. You know he was afraid of the President, too. All the older people were."

"But you made it all right with Delaney?" Mike persisted.

"Yes, of course. I only had to tell him what had happened to the chalice. He knew he would get it back."

"And he didn't mind about its having been broken?"

"No. He said it had been mended at that same place before."

She made no move as they went towards the door until Daly said softly:

"Good night, Sodia."

Then she got up for the first time since they had entered the room and came out into the hall with them. The sergeant had disappeared, but rumbles of laughter came up the stairs from the direction of the kitchen, showing that he was working his wiles on the Milligan's Mary.

Daly opened the front door to find Hamilton standing on the steps outside. He had a large square parcel under his arm and a large grin on his round face. He moved briskly into the hall, laid down his parcel and hung up his coat as if he owned the house. Then he held the front door firmly while he ushered Mike and Daly outside. Sodia stood in the background, looking a little dazed. When the door had shut behind them, Daly said with a little sigh:

"Hamilton will look after her. Why didn't I think of chocolates?"

"Too obvious," said Mike. "I'm thinking of whiskey. The time has come for you to lead me to 'The Cow'."

12

Long afterwards, Mike remembered how silent Daly was as they walked to "The Cow". He had been glad of the silence, because it gave him time to think about the Milligans, and Hamilton, and Bradley's strange generosity in paying for the repairs to the chalice. He wondered what could have been the reason for this. In a man to whom money was of the first importance, it could have been the impulse to pay in cash for good news. The good news might have been that now at last he had an excuse for getting rid of old Delaney. No one could blame him for retiring Delaney if it were known that he had become careless about the property of the College museum. Mike remembered, too, how Delaney had turned away when Bradley had come into the coffee-room on that first evening, as if Bradley had brought him to a sense of his own oddity, and he had hated Bradley for it. Professor Daly had told Mike about Delaney's remark that he had one important task to finish before he would be ready to retire. What if Bradley had become an obstacle to this, and Delaney had poisoned him to ensure that he would be left in peace? Immediately after this thought came another, that the cause of Milligan's uneasiness could be that he had manufactured nitro-benzene for his friend, Delaney. This was a remarkably trim-fitting theory. Milligan need not have known that the poison was for Bradley, since Delaney could have said that he wanted it for rats. But here Mike remembered with a slight shock that Professor Daly had told him how Delaney had described Bradley as a rat.

At that moment Daly said bitterly:

"Must you suspect my two oldest friends?"

"Who?"

"Delaney and Milligan, of course. That is what you are visibly churning over in your mind, isn't it? You think that Delaney and Milligan, having both been threatened with the same fate as Bradley, got together to poison him. You think that Milligan manufactured nitro-benzene and Delaney administered it. You have a vision of the two of them trotting off to gaol together, haven't you? Well, I can tell you at once that it is impossible."

"I'm very pleased to hear that," said Mike gently. "Just tell me why."

"Milligan would never have trusted Delaney to carry the nitro-benzene without spilling it," said Daly triumphantly. "You saw Delaney with a cup of coffee."

"He didn't spill it when I saw him," Mike reminded him.

"Not that time, perhaps. But usually he does. No one knows better than Milligan that if Delaney spilled nitro-benzene on his clothes, he would almost certainly die. I looked it up in the library while you were talking to Mrs. Bradley. If Delaney spilled nitro-benzene on the front of his waistcoat—and let me tell you, Delaney spills everything on the front of his waistcoat —he would inhale the vapour of the poison and die within twenty-four hours. Even if Delaney were not such a renowned spiller of liquids, you can take it from me that Science men have no respect whatever for Arts men. They hardly believe us capable of taking an aspirin to cure a cold. And there is another point."

"Well?"

"Delaney has been unhappy under Bradley. Milligan knew this. If the whole thing were Delaney's idea and he had asked Milligan for the poison, would it not have occurred to Milligan that Delaney really wanted it for himself?"

"Would that have stopped Milligan from giving it to him?"

"Yes," said Daly. "Besides, Delaney would have been incapable of administering poison to Bradley without letting Bradley know what he was about."

They were silent again as they walked past the long wall of the College park, until they came to the little bridge over the Styx. They paused in the middle of the bridge to look back towards the lighted College buildings. The wall ended here so that there was a clear view.

"I wish we had been able to avert this misfortune," said Daly after a moment. "Contact with reality is bad for universities. I wish it need not have happened."

"It was Bradley's own fault that it did," said Mike. "A really good President would have been more careful not to have had himself murdered."

"Bradley was incapable of being objective about his own fate," said Daly. "I spent an hour with him yesterday afternoon, trying to persuade him to go away. But he kept on doing Julius Caesar—'Shall Caesar send a lie,' and so on—until I saw that it was no use. It wasn't nobility, or courage, or devotion to duty that prevented him, either. I think he had an idea that he was safe as long as he stayed inside the College. And as he told me on the very evening that I arrived in the College, he felt quite capable of blackmailing whoever was threatening him. He only wished to be sure of blackmailing the right person. Don't be so distressed." He placed a solicitous hand on Mike's sleeve. "Presidents always blackmail their staffs. How else could they control them?"

Keeping his hand on Mike's arm, Daly moved on again. There were grassy banks on either side of the road now. In this backwater they might have been in the deep country, but for the widely spaced street lights. Then, just beyond a curve in the road they saw "The Cow". It was a long, low house, with a square porch jutting out without apology in the middle. From a sign above the door, a stout black cow leered knowingly down at the customers as they went in. Daly looked at his watch.

"Almost closing-time," he said. "Biddy is very punctual about shutting the door. We had better get inside quickly."

The porch was empty, but there was an inner door through which they could hear a murmur of voices. Daly pushed the door open, with an anticipatory grin, and Mike followed him into the bar.

It was dimly lit by two red-shaded hanging lamps. Behind the long worn counter that ran across the back of the room, a stout elderly woman was drying glasses in a leisurely way, with a snow-white linen cloth. A thin, small man of the same age was opening bottles and pouring stout into glasses for the solid line of customers who sat on tall wooden three-legged stools at the bar. This man's head was continually jerking to the right, as if his left ear was accustomed to being unexpectedly boxed. The floor was flagged with limestone, polished black by generations of boot-soles. An open turf fire at one end of the room was surrounded by grandmother chairs, each supporting a satisfied customer. Benches ran along the other walls, with small tables at intervals in front of them. Many of the occupants of the benches preferred to keep their glasses in greater safety clutched between their feet on the floor.

There was a pause in the conversation when Mike and Daly came into the room. Then there was a scuffle at the end opposite to the fireplace and a clear young voice said distinctly:

"Japers! It's the President!"

Three dim figures darted through another door, shutting it with a rattle of bolts. Laughter and conversation broke again. Mildly curious, Daly looked towards the door and then advanced to a free place at the end of the counter, saying:

"Good evening, Biddy."

"Good evening, sir," said Biddy heartily. She leaned confidentially over the counter. "And I heard you're made President, Professor. I thought we wouldn't see you in here no more."

"Only acting President, Biddy," said Daly, "and I laid down as a condition of taking it that I wouldn't have to change over to milk."

He introduced Mike to Biddy, who leaned across to shake his hand. Then she reached for two pottery tankards and filled them to overflowing with stout. Placing one in front of each of them, she said:

"There's a pint of the black cow's milk to mark Mr. Kenny's first visit, and the first appearance of a President in this bar. I hope you won't be spoiling my trade on me, President," she said in a low voice. "You know I conduct a good house, no alcohol for anyone under eighteen, no spirits until after the degree, maximum of three pints a man and then an hour's rest——"

"I know, I know," said Daly. "I wouldn't have come at all only that I wanted to bring Mr. Kenny." The old clock on the wall struck the half-hour. Daly went on hurriedly: "Anyway, it's closing-time now, and you know I couldn't possibly drink a pint of Guinness at my age—good night, Mike!" he finished suddenly, and walked quickly out by the way that they had come in, leaving Mike speechlessly clutching the handle of his tankard.

Biddy gave a little satisfied sigh and looked after him with affection.

"Always such a gentleman," she said complacently to Mike. "One hint is enough. Not that I liked asking him to go, but sure, I couldn't have the President of King's College perched on a stool at my bar. 'Twouldn't be fitting nor right. Undignified. And I wouldn't have a customer left after three days of it."

She raised her voice and said in a loud monotone:

"Closing-time, gentlemen, everyone is travellers I suppose, hop over and pull down the blinds, Mattie, and lock the door."

Everyone watched indulgently while Mattie came around from behind the bar and performed these tasks. When they turned back to their drinks again there was an increased air of intimacy and comfort in the room, as if they were all members of a benevolent though secret society. Mike took a long pull of his stout, hoping that Biddy would not discover that she was nursing a viper in her bosom, in the person of himself. Biddy seemed to have forgotten him. She was trotting briskly around the end of the counter to the door through which three of her customers had disappeared.

"Yez can come out now," she called. "He's gone."

The bolts were rattled again, the door creaked open and out came James Tennyson-Smith, John Fahy and a somewhat weather-beaten young man whom Mike could not remember having seen before. Biddy did not seem surprised to find that Mike was acquainted with two of the young men already.

"Now you won't feel lonesome," she said comfortably. "You couldn't be long coming here without getting to know Kid-

123

ney," she smiled indulgently at the third student. "He's like a son to me. His name is not really Kidney. We call him that because it's what always banjaxes him at the examinations."

She slipped agilely around behind the bar again and looked at them expectantly, her hands spread on the counter.

"My nerves could do with a little steadying after that contretemps," said the young man called Kidney. He rummaged in his pockets and produced four pennies and two half-pennies which he laid in a row on the counter. "Would that rise to a medium?" he asked hopefully.

"This will be on me," said Mike quickly, finishing his drink. "Now we'll all start level. You know what they like, Biddy."

The three young men thanked him perfunctorily, like children who have been given sweets. Then John Fahy said:

"For God's sake don't tell my mother, Mr. Kenny. I'm not really a confirmed drunkard yet."

His round face shone with earnestness. Kidney sighed and said lugubriously:

"Alas for me, I am."

Tennyson-Smith was silent and dull and it was plain that what thoughts he could achieve were engaged somewhere else. Mike watched him out of the corner of his eye and thought he discerned the hunted look of a young man about to run away and join the Foreign Legion. Biddy placed a pint of porter in front of Kidney and a mixture of beer and lemonade before each of the other two. Tennyson-Smith looked disparagingly at his and said:

"I'll have a double brandy."

"Faith and soul you won't," said Biddy cheerfully as she handed Mike another pint of porter. She moved away to register the price of the drinks on an old cash register with bells.

Kidney raised his glass to heaven and took a long drink. He put down the glass and turned to gaze at Mike as he said:

"Didn't I see you in the restaurant this evening with our honoured acting President, to flee from whose watchful eye we had to scoot into Biddy's kitchen?"

"That's right," said Mike.

John Fahy pulled at Kidney's sleeve and whispered sibilantly into his ear. Kidney looked at Mike again with greatly increased respect. John said:

"There's no secret about it now, Mr. Kenny, I suppose?"

"No," said Mike drily, "except for the awkward little fact that it's after closing-time."

"Don't mention that word," said Kidney sharply. "I should explain that we are conducting a philosophical experiment here. We hope that by ignoring the existence of—the phenomenon that you mentioned—it will be forced to cease to exist. As you see, we have already had a great measure of success. I'm afraid we may have suffered a setback this evening, since both yourself and the acting President mentioned—it."

"Sorry," said Mike meekly. "I didn't know."

"You couldn't have," said Kidney handsomely. "And you can understand that we can't put up a notice about it. Tell me, Mr. Kenny, are you here on business or pleasure? I hope you are leaving no stone unturned in your efforts to discover who murdered our President. We don't like that sort of thing in the College."

Mike assured him that he was leaving no stone unturned.

"Having the President murdered makes everyone very uneasy," said Kidney seriously. "Why, it might be a student next."

They had not noticed that Biddy had moved up behind the counter until she was level with them again. Now suddenly she leaned across the counter until her head was among them and looked eagerly from one to another.

"The President murdered?" she said. "Did you say murdered? And no one told me! There's gratitude, Kidney, after all the years I ran you through your physiology book, for all the good it did you. That Professor Badger was in a while back and he said the police were in the College about the President's death, but I thought 'twas only that there would be an inquest because he died sudden."

"Not so loud, please," said Kidney. "We don't want the whole mob discussing a family affair."

There was a pause while they listened to a loud argument about the breeding of greyhounds. The big man in the gaberdine coat who sat with his back firmly turned on Mike droned out for the fourth time:

"I say that Mutton Cutlet was overbred. There's Cutlets in every parish in Ireland after him."

"They're not listening," said Biddy. She hitched herself closer, so that Mike thought her feet must be swinging clear of the floor as she hung across the counter to whisper confidentially: "When you said murder, do you know who ran into my head at once? Professor Daly, that was in here a few minutes ago!"

"What about him?" asked Kidney. "He wouldn't hurt a fly."

"Do you mean that he may have killed the President so that he could be acting President?" asked John Fahy innocently.

"You may laugh," said Biddy heavily. "You may jeer and sneer and jib, but Professor Daly is a man that had a very good reason for wanting to see President Bradley under the sod."

She said this with such conviction that Mike felt as if he had always known its truth. He remembered immediately that the sergeant had said Daly looked like a man who had something to hide. Mike felt himself clutched in the grip of a primitive urge, like the instinctive craft of a hunting cat. He said carelessly:

"Why should Professor Daly wish Bradley dead? I thought they were great friends."

"On the outside, maybe," said Biddy. "But it's not everyone that knows that Mrs. Bradley was married to Professor Daly for three years, until one day Bradley came and took her away."

"Took her away?"

"Yes. You see, the way of it was that she thought Bradley was dead—guzzled by a mine in Africa or something—and she came home a poor widow and married Professor Daly. But after a while the bold Bradley came home, too, and demanded her back. Now, wouldn't that annoy a saint? Who'd blame Professor Daly for doing in the man that took his wife off him—a great housekeeper she was, too."

"How long ago did this happen?" Mike asked as soon as he

could frame a coherent question out of the many that tumbled about in his brain.

The students were silent now, as if they felt themselves in the presence of something beyond their understanding. Biddy calculated rapidly on her fingers.

"I suppose it must be twenty-five years," she said.

"That's a long time," said Mike gently.

"The mills of God grind slowly," said Biddy, "but they grind exceeding small. Maybe Professor Daly got brooding about it after he retired. I suppose he doesn't have much else to do below in Galway."

It was clear from her disparaging tone that she thought Galway was a desert. Now she was peeping eagerly up at Mike to see the effect of her information. Suddenly a wave of rage seemed to sweep over Kidney, for he shot out an arm as if he intended to knock Biddy off the counter. Mike seized his wrist in time, and forced his hand down by his side again. John Fahy's face had gone white. Tennyson-Smith had stepped back a pace. Kidney's lips were drawn back in a snarl. He spoke in a low monotone, all the more charged with venom for its apparent restraint:

"I know you now, Miss Macnamara. I don't believe your name is Biddy at all. You use false friendship and a cunning, seductive air to lure in your prey. You are a character, a good sort. You'll play stage-Irish if anyone brings a foreign visitor into your pub. Behind that you think you can be as mean-souled and as grasping as you like. But I see it all in your eyes —your spite against an innocent old man, because you don't want him here any more——"

"That's enough," said Mike sharply. "Come along now. We'll all be going."

Biddy's face was purple with indignation, but she had not yet found her voice. Mike hustled the three young men before him to the door. As he swung it open, the voice of the big man in the gaberdine coat boomed out:

"Cutlets in every parish in Ireland after him!"

13

Outside, the night air restored a feeling of sanity to them all. Mike realized that the young man called Kidney was shaking.

"What is your real name?" he asked.

"Thomas Finlay."

"Never submit to being called Kidney again," said Mike. "Do you realize how close you have gone to becoming a character yourself?"

"I'll never be able to go to 'The Cow' again," said Finlay mournfully. "No more sitting by the fire there in the winter evenings, with my books——"

"Don't you think that this will mean you will be able to pass your examinations?" said Mike.

"Oh-me-oh-my, all the same," said Finlay. "I suppose I knew it would have to end some day. But to see it suddenly as I did now, how cruel she is and what a fake—that was a shock, that was."

"I always knew she was a fake," said John Fahy mildly. "I watched her this morning getting old Lewis drunk and then trying to pump out of him what was happening in the College. She didn't get much change out of Lewis, though."

"You knew? Then why didn't you tell me?" Finlay demanded.

"Because you said she was like a mother to you," said Fahy without expression.

As long as he was in the company of the three young men Mike could not properly realize the implications of what Biddy had said. Finlay's disillusion was like a minor version of his own feeling that the whole world had slipped a cog and was hanging precariously over a bottomless chasm. Finlay's naïve and childish attack on Biddy had been a lesson to Mike, if he had needed it, on the futility of giving way to instinctive reaction. He wished that Finlay had held his peace, because Biddy just then had been eager to supply information, true or false, about everyone. Mike thought she had probably guessed that he was a policeman, and that she had been anxious to curry favour with him. Finlay's voice broke in on his thoughts.

"I'm afraid I made an ass of myself just now. You're not going to believe what a woman like that says, I hope."

"I think you're too hard on her," said Mike. "You go from one extreme to the other. Publicans often become ham actors as a sideline, to stimulate trade. After all, she's an uneducated old woman."

"*Touché*," said Finlay, after an uncomfortable pause.

Suddenly Tennyson-Smith came to life.

"That was very interesting, what she said about Mrs. Bradley," he said, stuttering in his eagerness. "That's the sort of thing people commit murder for, isn't it, Mr. Kenny?"

"I can think of other motives," said Finlay menacingly.

"Really," said Tennyson-Smith, "there is no need to use that tone to me. I'm simply trying to be objective——"

"Oh, run away and play!" said Finlay rudely.

"Good night, Mr. Kenny!" said Tennyson-Smith, outraged.

He turned around and marched off down a side street.

"He'll have to come back," said Fahy, still detached. "That is a cul-de-sac."

"Why were you so rude to him?" Mike asked Finlay.

"He confided to me that he fears that Professor Milligan murdered the President," said Finlay with contempt. "He doesn't care a hang about that, but he says he won't marry a murderer's daughter, and yet he fears that Miss Milligan will not easily release him from his promises to her."

"So they were engaged to be married?"

"He says so. He says she pursued him and I'm afraid there is a little truth in that. He's a vulgar, unchivalrous fellow to have discussed her at all."

Mike wondered about Finlay, how a man of such strong and high principles had fallen into such idle habits.

The College gates were just closing when they reached them.

As Mike walked up the avenue with the two young men, John Fahy said with respect:

"Then it's true that the Law never sleeps."

"Not quite," said Mike, and he gave no more information.

He entered the main hall with them and saw them mount the secondary stairs that led to the students' rooms before starting up the main stairs to look for Daly.

A line of light under the outer door showed that Daly was inside. He opened the door wide in answer to Mike's knock and said with a kind of lunatic heartiness:

"Come in, come in. It's never too late to be visited by a friend. I was just thinking about the word 'study', how sensitive we are about it. And yet Shakespeare has it: 'Get me a taper in my study, boy.' I always say 'study', do you?"

Suddenly he seemed to fade out, like a lamp whose oil-tank has dried up. Then he said, a little shakily:

"I see that I was right about Biddy. She is a regular mine of information, don't you think? Oh, come along in, for heaven's sake!"

He stumped across the room leaving Mike to come in and close the door as best he might. He stood against the dark background of the curtains, with his head down, looking up from under his eyebrows. Mike advanced cautiously to the fire and said:

"Why didn't you tell me about your association with Mrs. Bradley long ago? I wish I could have deprived Biddy of the pleasure of surprising me. She doesn't like you."

"I know," said Daly, looking a little smug. "One of my students used to go to her pub and write down her remarks in a little notebook. His heart was big with the wish for to be like James Joyce, but I put a stop to that by telling him she was laying it on. Somehow she found out about it. And then there was the little business of the verse I composed about her. It went like this." He raised his voice a semitone and droned it out:

> "Oh, sweetest Biddy of The Cow,
> The years sit lightly on thy brow,
> And though thy form is short and curvy,
> We know it's not from drinking Murphy."

"To me that sounds rather complimentary," Mike murmured.

"She didn't think so," said Daly. "It seems she had been trying to reduce. She gave up stocking Murphy's stout after that. A kind friend repeated the verse to her."

"But you still continued to go there?"

"Yes. I thought she had forgiven and forgotten. But it seems I was wrong." He sighed. "I think I actually wanted her to tell you about Helen. It was sure to come out sooner or later. Now you think I murdered Bradley to get her back, or from motives of revenge?"

"Well, no," said Mike gently. "I was rather wondering whether it could have been the other way around, that Mrs. Bradley murdered her husband to get you back."

"Ha!" said Daly with a snort. "It takes two to play that game!"

Mike sat down carefully in an armchair by the fire. Daly crossed to sit opposite him, and leaned over to put a fresh log on the fire. The sparks flew up with a crackle. Mike said after a moment:

"Mrs. Bradley was not happy with her husband. Indeed I doubt if even Bradley's cat could have been happy with him. He was self-satisfied, mean about money, a bully, and very exacting in his demands. I suggest that while you were on the staff here, she was content enough, because she saw you every day, but that after you retired she found her lot increasingly painful. I think it possible that your return brought things to a head, and that she decided to kill her husband and take the chance that you would receive her back."

"You flatter me," said Daly, but his expression was not as flippant as his words seemed to show. After a moment he went on: "I hope that it did not happen like that. I can't believe that it could. Besides, she and Bradley were only back in Dublin for a year before I retired."

"A year might be long enough," Mike said gently.

Daly said, rather hurriedly:

"I know she did not care for Bradley, but she always had a great sense of duty. I doubt if she would be capable of killing

131

him, not matter how much he deserved it. And she is very religious. Bradley had a religion once, but as he confided in someone, he only found it a hindrance, so he gave it up. Helen would not have cut him off with all his imperfections on his head without giving him a chance of repentance. In fact, she was too religious to be capable of murder at all. I knew her very well, as you may imagine."

"Tell me all about it," said Mike, who had listened with a deep sense of relief to these remarks.

Daly leaned back in his chair and closed his eyes. It was clear that the recollection was sharply painful to him, though it was all so long ago.

"I knew Helen since she was at school," he said after a moment. "She is sixteen years younger than I am. She was only two years younger than Bradley. She married Bradley when she was twenty-two. She had spent the intervening years at home looking after the house for her mother who was something of a tyrant. Her life didn't change much in that respect, poor girl. I was at the wedding. I was on the staff here at the time and I had known Bradley as a student. Milligan gave you a good picture of him as he was then."

"I remember," said Mike. "What did he look like? No one has mentioned that."

"Rather elegant, curiously enough," said Daly. "He was thinner then. But he had a calculating expression which I did not care for, and he was ordering poor Helen around immediately after the ceremony. She had a little income of her own and I remember thinking even then that it was for this he had married her.

"Well, they went off to South Africa, via a honeymoon in France and southern Italy. Bradley had a job of some kind—Helen's mother was vague about everything except that in future she would have to look after her household herself. She complained to everyone at the wedding of Helen's selfishness in getting married at all. Oh, it was a typical wedding and no mistake.

"Well, time passed, and after about seven years Helen arrived home, and we were told that Bradley was dead. He had gone out with a party to inspect a mine and he had disappeared. There was some sort of an explosion, and later pieces of a man were found, and everyone decided that it was Bradley, damaged beyond repair. It must have been some unfortunate tramp who had sheltered near the mine. They never found out who he was, except that he was not Bradley. Bradley had gone off with a little bit of fluff, never intending to be away for more than a month or two. What was his rage to find when he came home that his wife, instead of waiting patiently for him as she should have done, had cleared off home to Ireland in the most callous fashion. He didn't hurry himself to follow her. It was four years later before he appeared in Dublin again, and in the meantime Helen had married Auld Robin Grey."

"I beg your pardon?"

"She had married me," said Daly, with his first sign of impatience. "We were married very quietly. Her mother was there, lamenting that just when her daughter had come back and everything was going nicely again, someone else had to come along and take her away. We set up house in Ballsbridge, not far from the Royal Dublin Society's showgrounds."

Mike asked a question to which he had been longing to know the answer, for the fearful complications that might follow.

"Were there any children?"

"Fortunately, no," said Daly, and he raised an exasperated eyebrow at Mike, seeing at once the relief that flooded over him.

"Please go on," said Mike.

"Three years after we were married we were sitting in our front garden one sunny day in August. I remember I had just got up to cut the withered heads off some roses, when I noticed a man peering over the hedge of the garden. Well, that was one of the things I hated most about marriage and suburban life— being peered at over the hedge. Most unnerving, I always found it. I got quite angry and I went across to tell the fellow to go about his business. Then I saw that it was Bradley. I remember that I felt very little surprise. 'Fancy that,' I said to him. 'We all thought you were dead. So glad to find you're not.' He made no answer, but just stood staring across the garden at Helen. She hadn't seen him yet. 'That's my wife you have there,' he said, quite rudely. 'Well, then, why don't you take her away?' I said, and I just went on cutting the heads off the roses."

"Is that all you said?" Mike asked in awe.

"Well, I must admit that I succumbed to the temptation to quote *Enoch Arden* at him—you remember that beastly fellow who had such a fancy for nuts in his youth and who got cast away on a desert island?"

"I remember," said Mike.

"I have often wondered whether Tennyson ever ate nuts himself," said Professor Daly meditatively. "He was awfully glib about them. But then he was always writing about things he knew nothing of—sitting up there in the Manor with a well-sprung armchair under his fanny, writing away about desert islands and village revels and waking and calling me early, call me early, Mother dear. Can you remember the name of Enoch's nut-cracking sweet? Annie, or Ellen, or Maggie or some such suitable name——"

"No," said Mike, with awful calm. "I do not remember. Is that the whole story? Is that all that happened?"

"Well, almost," said Daly, returning reluctantly to reality. "You see, as I think I mentioned, Helen had a great sense of duty. As soon as she looked up and saw Bradley, she rose to the occasion just as you would expect. She asked him in and she sent for some tea. Yes, I remember that she got some tea for him. Then presently she went away with him."

"Just like that?"

"Why not? We had only a monthly tenancy of the house, so there was no trouble about that. She went back to her mother's place for a week or two and then she went off to Africa again, or somewhere like that, with Bradley. I'm not very clear about that part of it. I'm afraid I rather lost touch."

"And where did you go?"

"I stayed with Milligan for a few weeks and I then moved back into these rooms again. Mrs. Milligan was very good to me. Milligan just said he had always warned me not to have anything to do with Bradley. We understood each other."

"So you just went straight back to your old way of life?" Mike persisted, as if some force outside of himself were compelling him to try to discover Daly's philosophy.

The old man looked at him sharply. Then he said:

"I have no feeling for property, no possessive instincts, except in the matter of my false teeth and my best suit, and possibly one or two books. Even those I know I must leave behind me when I die. I was not young when I married Helen. I was a great deal older when I was released from bondage. Now, don't misunderstand me. She is a very excellent woman and a first-rate housekeeper. She was always cheerful and willing, and decorative, too, though you might not think so to look at her now. But she never read a book. She said she *preferred* the *Saturday Evening Post* and the *Ladies' Home Journal*. She never went to concerts. She said *everyone* at a symphony concert was there for the sole purpose of being seen by everyone else. She could not tell me how it all began, but she was quite sure of this, all the same. Since we both hold with Rome, we were doomed to agreeing to differ on most philosophical points until death would us part. When Bradley came along we hailed him as a fairy godmother——"

"Perhaps you did," said Mike. "But can you be so certain about Mrs. Bradley?"

Again Daly looked worried, but he said:

"Oh, she didn't mind. She was a sensible woman."

Still Mike was sure that she had minded and had probably been terribly hurt at the ease with which Daly had discarded her. Mike knew that under Daly's cultivated detachment there was a layer of what would have been selfishness in anyone else. In him it was devotion to learning, so strong that any hindrances would be ruthlessly thrust aside. Mrs. Bradley, without a doubt, had been a hindrance, but he would never have thrust her aside if the opportunity had not offered. Once it had, however, Daly would have considered that he would be flying in the face of Providence if he refused.

"Stop there!" said Daly, who had been watching Mike's face. "There's no need for you to understand fully."

135

"Just one more question," said Mike humbly. "Was there ever any suggestion of a charge of bigamy against her?"

"No. I never really understood why, unless it is that Bradley prevented it. Bradley would have hated law-courts, even at that early stage of his career. I can't think who else would have bothered. I know you can't bear to think of things like this not being brought tidily into court," he added kindly, "but I really can't tell you why it wasn't done. Perhaps it was because the country was still a little upset at that time."

Silence fell between them while Mike turned the whole astonishing story over and over in his mind. Then Daly said:

"Helen would not have used nitro-benzene, by the way. A barbiturate, perhaps, if she had had one in the house, or the gas cunningly left on in a corner of the bedroom—something simple and direct. But I must insist that her principles would not have allowed her to murder anyone, least of all her husband. Besides, she may not have been as unhappy with Bradley as you think. He was far more her type than I was—he would never have wanted her to improve her mind with reading, or music, or any of that sort of thing, because he didn't care for those things himself."

Mike leaned back carefully in his chair, suddenly overwhelmed with an idea so neat that it took his breath away.

"Badger," he brought out after a struggle. "I must see Badger." He looked at his watch and groaned. "Ten minutes past eleven. I have no excuse for breaking in on him at this hour of the night——"

"Think nothing of that," said Daly. "I'll just telephone to let him know we're coming."

"But he'll be going to bed——"

"No, no. He sleeps by day. Don't you know *any* natural history? He'll be starting to work now, as he always does, though come to think of it, I haven't seen his name in print for years. He won't like being disturbed, but we'll tell him he can't hold up the course of justice."

"But Mrs. Badger—what about her?"

"She doesn't sleep much. She can't afford to."

Struck dumb by this cryptic remark, Mike waited while

Daly trotted off down to the public telephone in the hall. Not for the first time since the beginning of their friendship he was astonished at Daly's humility. Mike believed that it was this humility which had led him into the error of thinking that Mrs. Bradley could be satisfied with Bradley's company after having enjoyed his own. He had seemed quite sincere in seeing no reason for complaint on her part. Surely the measure of her devotion had been that she had said not one word about her marriage to Daly in the course of her conversation with Mike. Mike's heart was wrung for the sufferings of professors' wives. How adaptable they had to be, and how agile. Of course they did not all have to submit to being swapped around like Mrs. Bradley. But they all needed the devotion and concentration of lion-tamers to keep their charges healthy and contented. Mike had not failed to notice how few of the King's College professors were married. The reason obviously was that the College provided such comfortable rooms and service, that no wife could hope to compete with them. Mike found himself thinking of his linoleum-floored lodgings and motherly land-lady with distaste.

"That's all fixed up," said Daly briskly, coming back into the room. "There is a little snag in the way of supper-hospitality offered, but you must be prepared to suffer something in the cause of duty. To horse, boot and saddle!"

Suddenly realizing that he was desperately tired, Mike heaved himself upright and followed Daly downstairs.

14

The front gates were locked when they reached them, but Daly opened the wicket with a key which he carried in his pocket.

"I very prudently kept the key when I retired," he explained. "You never can tell when a thing like that will be useful."

Badger lived a quarter of an hour's walk away from the College, in the direction of the city. The house was large and ramshackle, standing in an enclosed garden with a high wall that ran along by the road.

"Poor old Badger suffers a good deal from his children," said Daly. "They run wild around the garden and ambush visitors as they come in through the gate. They build houses in the trees and wigwams on the lawn, and insist on spending the night in them. They suffer from every fixation and inhibition known to man. I should say that they will make remarkable adults, but at present they are more than trying. Fortunately they will be in bed now."

A light showed in a large window beside the front door. Daly sighed a little in anticipation of Mrs. Badger's supper, and rang the bell. There was the sound of a door opening and then the voices of the Badgers could clearly be heard from the hall.

"You open it," said Badger.

"No, you open it," said Mrs. Badger. "He's your professor."

"I will not open it," said Badger. "And, anyway, he's your policeman!"

"What exactly do you mean by that?" Mrs. Badger demanded. "Open that door this instant!"

"I will not," said Badger. "You open it."

Daly hammered thunderously on the panels of the door and shouted:

"Open up, in the name of the Law!"

There was dead silence inside for a moment. Then a door banged. They could hear heavy breathing. A light was switched on inside and now Mike understood why every sound had come out so clearly, for a long line of light showed at one side of the door where the wood had warped. Then at last the door was opened and there was Mrs. Badger with a smile that looked just a trifle fixed.

"I'm afraid I kept you waiting," she said. "I didn't hear the bell at first."

She took their overcoats and threw them on the back of a chair. Professor Daly's eyes narrowed with pain as he saw the plight of his beloved Blarney tweed. But he was too polite to protest, and he followed Mrs. Badger into the drawing-room with his air of resignation redoubled.

It was a large square room, so sparsely furnished that it looked even larger than it was. The floor was bare boards, except for a carpet which was meant for a much smaller room, and which served as a hearthrug here. The furniture was chipped and battered, and showed clearly by its condition that it was often pushed into unnatural positions for the purpose of building hide-outs on wet days. There were books everywhere, and various Florentine notabilities grinned sardonically down on the Badgers from the relative safety of the walls. There was an Adam chimney-piece, festooned with nude marble ladies who were probably glad of the warmth of the large coal fire that burned beneath them.

At one side of the fire, facing the door, Badger sat in an armchair glooming up at them through his sandy eyebrows and clutching the *Times Literary Supplement* into a crumpled agony between his hands. Daly stepped across quickly and took it from him, smoothed it out as best he could and laid its battered remains to rest on top of one of the bookshelves. Then he said genially:

"Nice evening, Badger. You met Mr. Kenny at dinner last night."

While Badger shook Mike's hand without enthusiasm, Mrs. Badger said:

"I guessed last night that you were not a vocational school inspector. You put up quite a good show, but you couldn't look like a teacher. They are unmistakable, really. Do sit down. I'll just get supper."

Mike sat on the sofa facing the fire and Daly settled himself comfortably in the armchair on his left. Mike said:

"I'm sorry for calling so late. Professor Daly says you don't go to bed early."

"That is true," said Badger with quiet pride. "I find I work better by night."

They talked about Badger's habits until the door opened and Mrs. Badger pushed in a trolley whose wheels squealed so loudly that no further conversation was possible until they were silent. Then they had supper of weak bottled coffee, utterly tasteless, of Mrs. Badger's own economical one-egg boiled porter-cake, and of her special biscuits made of cornflakes and melted chocolate. Professor Daly moaned gently as he drank his coffee, but otherwise he did not complain. Even if he had wished to do so, Mike could not have begun to discuss Bradley's death, because Mrs. Badger kept up a loud discourse on every subject possible, from the recipes of her abominable cakes to her difficulties in bringing up her children. Her voice rose higher and higher, until Daly and Mike both began to fear that she was on the brink of a fit of hysterics. Then Badger suddenly took charge. He sat up straight on the edge of his chair and emitted one word:

"Mother!"

She collapsed slowly, like a motor tyre with a minor puncture. Badger kept his eye on her until he was sure that she was quite flat. Then he said:

"You can clear away now."

Meekly she collected their cups and squealed her trolley out of the room.

"Now," said Badger, sitting back in his chair again, "I know what brought you here. Fox told you I was looking through letters in the President's office."

"That is so," said Mike.

"Things are never as simple as they look," said Badger earnestly. "Each factor must be examined carefully before a solution is reached. Never jump to the obvious conclusion. That must be understood before any progress can be made."

"There are one or two other things to be understood too," said Mike grimly. "One of them is that I dislike having the course of my enquiries hampered by irresponsible gossip. Everywhere I have been to-day you have been there before me, handing out inaccurate information, spreading panic, inducing quite innocent people to become secretive and frightened—why did you do that?"

"One has a sense of responsibility," Badger spluttered. "This is a very serious matter for the College——"

"I'm afraid it will be a serious matter for you," said Mike, "if it does not stop. Did you find them?"

"Find what?"

"The anonymous letters in the President's office."

"What are you talking about?"

"The anonymous letters that you wrote to the President about the Leahy money and various other things," Mike explained carefully. "You just thought you'd slip in and get them back before Daly would have had time to find them."

"Badger!" Daly sat up straight and looked at his old student in amazement. "*You* writing anonymous letters. I can't believe it."

"Why not?" Mike asked quickly.

"It's not true, anyway," said Badger.

"Why not?" Daly's voice rose to a squeak. "Because Badger never does anything anonymously. He's celebrated for the—for the reverse of anonymous letters! If Badger thinks a man is doing wrong, he seeks him out, seizes him by the lapel of his coat, backs him into a corner from which there is no escape, and tells him all about it with quotations from every philosopher from Saint Thomas Aquinas downwards. That is the secret of Badger's reputation. Isn't that so, Badger?"

"In my youth", Badger intoned, "I made the discovery that falsehood and insincerity were nibbling at the roots of society.

141

I determined then that I would never tolerate either of these vices, neither in myself nor in any of my associates. Not even when they are clothed in the guise of charity and toleration will I put up with them. These are only euphemisms for a dangerous liberalism which is hurling the world to destruction——"

"It's all right, Badger, old chap," said Daly kindly. "You are among friends now."

"He is no friend," said Badger, pointing a quivering, indignant forefinger at Mike. "He came here to arrest my wife!"

There was a little silence charged with shock. Then Badger's eyes grew suddenly round. They could see his mind swiftly leaping ahead through every point of the explanation that would have been necessary for an ordinary man. Then he gave a little tired shrug and said:

"Now that all is discovered I had better tell you the whole story."

"I should recommend that," said Daly, and Mike said:

"If you please."

They waited then, while Badger thought long lugubrious thoughts. Presently Mike was beginning to doubt whether he would be able to resist leaping upon Badger and clumping his head for him. Outwardly he succeeded in keeping an appearance of impenetrable calm, with his long, fine fingers just touching each other at the tips as he sat back easily on the sofa. His discomfort was increased by the fact that some small, hard object was making itself felt beneath him, but he feared to create a diversion by removing it. He occupied himself with trying to diagnose its shape. Was it a toy motor-car, or a lead soldier? Yes, a lead soldier, surely, with fixed bayonet, exacting revenge for his disturbance of the Badger household. It was just possible that it was a gunboat, however. Fortunately Badger's powers of speech returned to him just then, so that Mike was saved from further speculation.

"My wife is devoted to me," Badger began, waving a deprecating hand.

"Silly little woman," said Daly under his breath.

Fortunately Badger did not hear this. He went on:

"Perhaps I made a mistake in taking her into my confidence, but I have always done so, and I had no premonition that she would take it all so seriously."

"Take *what* so seriously?" asked Daly. "Explain yourself, man! Be clear and cogent, not cryptic."

Badger cocked a tired eye at him, but he did not seem offended as he said:

"When Bradley became President at first, as you have probably heard, he seemed to feel a special responsibility for the work of each member of the staff. He was never done reproaching them for lack of devotion to their work, accusing them of cutting lectures, urging them to wilder and more impossible feats of research. He seemed to want glory for himself, by way of the College. He reduced everyone to a state of nervous exhaustion, while he became every day more smug and fat and comfortable. He drove poor old Delaney quite mad, which I thought need never have happened."

"You think Delaney is really insane?" asked Mike, who had suddenly realized that for all his odd appearance and habits, Badger had a sharp, well-balanced mind.

"Yes, Delaney is quite insane now," said Badger. "He was a border-line case for a great many years, but that in a professor is scarcely noticeable." A gleam of humour lit up his cold eyes for a moment and was gone. "He was always able to lecture, and he dug up half the countryside in his zeal, but he was just a little cracked, and Bradley didn't like that. He destroyed Delaney's self-esteem and for that I can never forgive him."

"How?"

"He used to write to Delaney whenever any notability was coming to the College and ask him to stay out of sight that day." Mike could not restrain a slight exclamation of shock. "Yes, that was bad. Delaney has got it into his head that he must do the College one great service before retiring, so that everyone will have to admit his value. He is like a slighted child, awkwardly looking for his parents' attention. That, of course, is why he keeps on talking about rats. You may not know it, but Delaney sees rats when no one else does. He insisted to me

143

the other day that there was a procession of them marching two and two across the museum floor. There was nothing there, of course. Well, some months ago I went to see Bradley to tell him that I thought he was treating Delaney badly. I said I thought he was treating everyone badly, but that it was having a particularly bad effect in Delaney's case. I told him he had received his power from God, and that if he continued to misuse it in this fashion, God would doubtless make him pay for his fun in the next world. He got quite cross, I remember, and ordered me out. I wouldn't go, of course. I just repeated what I had said, with further embellishments. I refused to leave, in fact, until he had agreed to let Delaney alone.''

"And did he?" Daly asked, eyeing Badger with respect and clearly appreciating why Bradley had capitulated.

"He stopped annoying Delaney and he began on me," said Badger.

"Bradley was unconquerable, then," said Daly.

"He had more spirit than I had given him credit for," said Badger grudgingly. "Before I left that day I told him that I would call on him every week until I was sure that Delaney was safe from him. That put an idea into his head. Every few days he would send a message saying that he wanted to see me in his office. He knew my principles would not allow me to make a personal issue of our disagreement over Delaney. When I would arrive he would just look up blandly and say he had not sent for me at all. When this had happened three or four times I ignored the summons, and of course it turned out that he had a world-famous literary historian that I would have given my eye to meet, sitting over in his office waiting for me. It happened like that several times, until I hardly knew what I was doing, for brooding on it. What made it so galling was that Bradley loved celebrities and was delighted to have them all for himself. I complained about him to my wife, of course, and she was very sympathetic, as she always is. I said some wild things about Bradley—that he would like to get his hands on Leahy's money—that sort of thing, quite without foundation, just to relieve my feelings." He looked anxiously at Mike's face for comfort, but did not find it. Then he went on disconsolately: "What was my horror yesterday to find a document on my wife's writing-table, in her handwriting, listing these—crimes, and with a silly little drawing of a tombstone at the foot of the page, with Bradley's name on it. I saw at once what she was at, and I told her that she must not think of sending it. Only then did I discover that she had been sending—communications of this nature to Bradley for months past. One every week, she told me. She used to write it while she was preparing the laundry list, and post it late in the evening. She is a very methodical person."

"Evidently," said Mike without expression. "What did you do?"

"I'm afraid I rather lost my head," said Badger. "We were going to dinner with Bradley in the evening. There was nothing strange in that. Bradley believed in entertaining friend and foe impartially. I was not sure whether he was going to amuse himself by insulting me there, but I rather thought he wouldn't on account of Daly being present. He had a great respect for you, Daly, for some reason. He seemed anxious that you should approve of him."

"I have been known to produce that effect quite spontaneously," said Daly solemnly, "but in this case the explanation was that Bradley wanted me to help him to find out who was writing the letters, as we must call them, threatening his life."

"Threatening his life? Oh, you mean the tombstone," said Badger uneasily. "And Mrs. Badger is a graduate in science and a former student of Milligan's." His voice rose. "And we were at dinner with him and took part in that awful business of the biscuit——"

"Come back to what you did when you found out that your wife was threatening the President's life," said Mike firmly.

"She said she only wanted to frighten him," said Badger piteously. "She said that people like Bradley feel that they are exceptions to the general rule that we must all die, sooner or later. She said he was too healthy and had never had a proper fright to teach him respect for his fellowman. She said that after a few more weeks she had intended to send only one letter a fortnight, and then gradually to drop them altogether. I told her she had done a terrible thing, and though she couldn't help being pleased with herself, she agreed at last not to send any more. Then, this morning, we heard that Bradley was dead and Mrs. Badger said that I should try to get the letters back. She said that if the new President found them there might be trouble. If I had known that you would take over, Daly, I should probably not have bothered to burgle the office at all. I should simply have asked you for them."

"Did you find them?" Mike asked for the second time, and this time Badger answered:

"No. But I had not got very far when Foxy came along. Foxy is very righteous."

"What did you do when Fox came in?"

Badger looked uncomfortable.

"Oh, I just said I had been looking for the President, and Foxy said in a nasty way: 'He would hardly fit in the filing cabinet.' So I said I was looking for a letter I had written to Bradley and wanted to get back. I came away then because I could see it was no use trying any more that time. Really, Fox takes too much on himself." Badger's face reddened at the recollection. "He stood at the window with his hands under the tails of his coat, watching me go away, as if he thought I would try to duck back in again somehow——"

"No doubt you were a bit sensitive," Daly murmured, without any intention of being unkind.

"Where did you go last night after you left Bradley's house?" Mike asked, after a little pause.

"We walked home," said Badger. "You saw us go. We have no car. It takes a quarter of an hour to walk here from College. Why do you ask? What are you driving at?"

"Never mind," said Mike. He stood up briskly, his weariness forgotten and his long thin features alert and watchful as he said: "Do you care for music, Professor Badger?"

"Of course," said Badger, surprised at the abrupt change of subject. "We are both very fond of music."

"You go to concerts, then?"

"We manage to get to nearly every good concert."

"What part of the house do you favour?"

"The gods," said Badger sharply. "Has no one told you that we have seven children? They all like music, too, but we have had to make a rule never to bring more than two with us."

He looked at Mike with anxious, raised eyebrows, but Mike only thanked him for the information and started for the door. Daly got up slowly and began to follow him. Badger's expression showed the smug disillusion of a man who has been preaching disaster for years and who has at last been proved right. Daly looked at him anxiously and said:

"I would never have told Bradley if I had found out who was writing the letters."

"Thank you," said Badger, but he looked no happier.

When they came into the hall Mrs. Badger moved towards them from the gloom at the back.

"Must you go so soon?" she twittered, and stopped dead as if a hawk had got her in mid-song, as she caught sight of her husband's face.

Daly and Mike thanked her gravely for her hospitality, and then Badger let them out into the garden. Before they had time to move off the steps they heard the voices of the Badgers as clear as Sunday bells through the defective panels of the door.

"Did they know all about the letters?" asked Mrs. Badger in a dull, rasping voice.

"They knew some and I told them the rest," said Badger.

"*You* told them!"

"Yes. It's always better to do that," said Badger.

"There's one good thing anyway," said Mrs. Badger. "Nothing can bring Bradley back to life again. Put out the light."

Daly took Mike's elbow and marched him down the path to the gate. There they looked back and saw lights go on upstairs.

"Doesn't either of the Badgers *ever* say please?" Mike asked in awe.

"It would be a sign of weakness," said Daly. "Why didn't you arrest her?"

"Because Bradley, being dead, can't charge her with threatening his life," said Mike.

"Then you don't think she poisoned him?"

"No. But I think I know who did."

15

As they walked slowly back to the College Mike was fully taken up with answering Daly's clamorous questions. Daly would allow no careless logic and gradually Mike himself became more and more impressed with the inevitability of his theory. At last Daly said:

"Yes, that must be the explanation. I wonder how long it would all have continued if Bradley had not been poisoned."

"It should never have developed so far at all," said Mike severely.

"Now, now," said Daly, wagging his head, "I warned you that university people all live at one remove from life."

"Sometimes that gives them a very good view of what is happening," said Mike. "The best hurler is the man on the ditch. Your friend Badger is a clever man."

"I'm glad you see that." Daly was delighted with this tribute. "I have a great regard for Badger's ability. He's overwhelmed with his family just now, but in a few years' time he will develop still further."

"Won't he be a bit old then?" Mike asked doubtfully.

"Not at all. Forty is infantile for a professor."

Although it was long after midnight by the time they reached the College, almost every window was still lit up. It seemed to Mike that there was a slightly mad air about the way in which the lights streamed out across the grass, as if the people who inhabited the College took no cognizance of the ordinary laws of night and day. Or perhaps it was that they were like children who have not yet learned the conventions that rule the world. This same child-like quality seemed to keep them in a state of wonder, highly conducive to the pursuit of research but entirely useless in protecting them from their more scoundrelly colleagues, or in revealing plots. Like children, they expected everything to come out right in the end, and when it did not, they closed their eyes tight until they had succeeded in forgetting that evil existed in the world at all. No other community, Mike thought in exasperation, would have allowed itself to be gulled as this had been. He tried to express some of this to Daly, who nodded and said, a little smugly:

"Yes, we live like the blessed in Paradise, taking no thought for the morrow."

"There were snakes in Paradise, too," said Mike. "There should be a few Guards inside every University College in the country to protect the inmates from this kind of thing."

"Yes, it was too late when you arrived," said Daly, with a sigh. "By the way, I don't like that word, 'inmates'."

Lewis was in the little porters' office in the main hall when they went in. He looked pale, and he drooped slightly, but otherwise he seemed to have recovered from his morning's lapse. He came across to speak to them, trailing an evening paper on the floor as if to show the depth of his scorn for its contents.

"Did you see this rag, Professor?" He pointed down to it. "Our College is disgraced. Things will never be the same again. The President was a nuisance while he was alive, but he seems to be doing just as much harm now that he's dead." He dashed away a querulous tear that had splashed on to his chin. "People seem to be turning night into day—there was Professor Fox asking for you a few minutes ago, as cool as if it was midday instead of midnight. And that Guard is waiting in your study as if he owned it. I tried every means of getting him out, but he just wouldn't go——"

"It's all right, Lewis," said Daly soothingly. "You'll see that things will improve in a day or two."

"No, no, they'll get worse," Lewis insisted. "I know they will."

His whining voice followed them up the stairs as he stood in the hall looking after them.

Daly opened the study door. The sergeant was sitting motionless on a straight chair in the middle of the room. He seemed to have made no attempt to entertain himself with a book or newspaper while he waited. Such people always reminded Daly of cab-horses, or cattle at a fair, deriving adequate occupation from their own slow thoughts. The sergeant's face lit up when he saw Mike.

"I was afraid you might go home for a sleep, sir," he said. "I wanted to tell you how I spent the evening."

A word of invitation was enough to start him off on a long and close recital of Bradley's activities on the day of his death. A great part of the morning had been spent with Mr. Leahy. Porters from every part of the College could testify to the rage of their professors whose lectures had been interrupted so that Leahy could be shown the rooms. Burren, Donovan and Hamilton had mentioned to their students later that they were contemplating murdering Bradley. Burren's students had approached the sergeant, eagerly offering to lay a trap for him and deliver him up alive. They had been palpably disappointed when MacCarthy had refused.

Bradley had spent the afternoon at home as he usually did. Nellie had already told MacCarthy about the people who had called on him then, and he had brought her over the list again for closer details. First had come Professor Daly. He had stayed almost for an hour, and had been seen to the door by Bradley himself with remarkable cordiality. Miss Milligan had come next. She had arrived like a lion and gone out like a lamb, also ushered by Bradley himself. Nellie had observed these things through the open door of the dining-room where she had been laying the table for dinner. After Miss Milligan had left the President had come into the dining-room and told her that there would be two extra people for dinner.

The next person to whom Nellie had opened the door was Professor Delaney. He had seemed very excited and had said that he must see the President at once, on a very urgent matter connected with rats. He panted on her heels while she opened the study door to announce him, and darted in under her outstretched arm before she had time to speak. As she closed the door she heard him start off in a shrill monologue, interjected now and then with soothing noises from the President. She confessed without embarrassment that she had listened to the

151

fun for a moment before going back to her work. Delaney had been pleading to be allowed to try one final plan for exterminating the rats for good and all. When he paused for breath the President had seemed to be giving him his blessing, but Delaney had paid no attention. He had continued to pour out his tirade as if he had received no answer at all. Then Nellie had tired of it and had gone back to the dining-room.

"I wonder why Bradley didn't have in a firm of rodent exterminators," said Daly thoughtfully. "You know those fellows with bandy legs and knee-breeches so that the rats can hop between their knees. You give them the run of the building and they go all over it, into every nook and cranny, with a special gas. According to Delaney, Bradley would have had to keep out of their way."

Mike said:

"Yes, that would have satisfied Professor Delaney. But Bradley did not want people looking into every nook and cranny of the College. What was the end of that interview?"

MacCarthy said that it had taken the President about half an hour to soothe Delaney with promises and get him out of the house. Ten minutes after he had left, at about five o'clock, the doorbell had sounded again, and Nellie had let in Professors Hamilton and Fox together. Hamilton had waited in the hall while Fox went into the study. He had chatted to Nellie through the dining-room doorway in the most amiable fashion. Fox's interview had been a short one, for after no more than ten minutes he had come out alone and had let himself out of the house. Then Hamilton had gone into the study and a few minutes later Nellie, decorously polishing glasses, had heard him shouting at the President about Miss Milligan. She had been afraid to go closer to the door and listen, Nellie said, because that Professor Hamilton was a terror and he would have been sure to catch her. But she had heard Miss Milligan's name, and presently the President must have soothed him down, because they came out of the room arm in arm.

"Bradley was probably arm in arm, all right," Daly murmured, "but not Hamilton. Bradley had a beastly habit of handling people, God rest him."

That had been the last of the visitors, said MacCarthy, and Nellie had not seen the President again until dinner-time.

"Did he not take tea?" Daly asked.

"Yes," said MacCarthy, "he nipped out and had it in the drawing-room after Delaney had gone. Nellie said he never gave tea to visitors because he was too mean. She said he'd rather do without his own than give it to a visitor. And by the way, sir, I found out the other things you wanted to know, too. The first one is that Bradley had an overdraft of about seven hundred pounds."

"An overdraft!" Daly's shocked tone was almost ridiculous. "Are you sure?"

"I am, so," said MacCarthy. "He paid in his salary cheque every month and drew out more than he paid in—a very easy way for getting an overdraft."

"But we all thought Bradley was a wealthy man," Daly spluttered. "I told you that, Mike, didn't I? That was one of the reasons why they made him President—I told you——"

"That was the impression he wanted to give, certainly," said Mike, remembering Bradley's air of being mysteriously superior to everyone else. "Did he never have money?" he asked the sergeant.

"When he came back from Africa the last time he had about a hundred pounds, his bank manager says. That was nearly gone by the time he got the job here and he has lived from month to month since then. But last week he mentioned that he wanted to open a deposit account as well as his current account, and that he would call about it again in a few days."

"And have you checked where the people went after the dinner-party?"

"Yourself and Professor Daly came here," said MacCarthy woodenly. "Tennyson-Smith brought Miss Milligan home. The housekeeper let them in, and she says that they fought with each other until about two o'clock in the morning. She heard the front door banging when the young fellow went away. Perhaps he nipped back here and poisoned the President?" he finished hopefully. "I wouldn't mind arresting that fellow."

"It's not so easy to poison a President," Daly pointed out.

"You can't just say: 'Open your mouth and close your eyes,' and pop the poison in.'"

The sergeant was not amused.

"Professor Burren didn't get home until four in the morning, though he has rooms right here near us. It was the night watchman that told me that. The Badgers went home at once, but we don't know whether they got into bed and stayed there. I didn't question any of those professors. I told you I'd be afraid, remember?"

"So long as you got the information," said Mike soothingly. "What about the ticket?"

The sergeant opened a large envelope which he had been clutching and drew out the little piece of blue paper.

"You should have heard the language of the man that tested that for fingerprints," he said with satisfaction. "He wanted to know if it had been handed to every monkey in the zoo before he got it. He says there isn't a hope of learning anything from it."

"You'd be surprised," said Mike mildly, reaching for the ticket and putting it away in an inside pocket. "And the forged five-pound notes?"

"Tennyson-Smith gave two of them to a Grafton Street jeweller," said the sergeant, "and that's the first time that we have been able to tell where the money came from. I handled them myself and I'd say they're almost perfect. The fellow in the shop noticed that the lady on one of them had a little squint and he showed it, innocent-like, to another fellow. The two of them were laughing over them hearty when the boss came along and he didn't see anything to laugh at. There's terrible excitement over them in the office—I was down there for a few minutes a while ago. I told them to send a few extra lads up here, in case we'd be needing them."

"Good man. Have they come yet?"

"Not yet. This place is like a flea circus," said the sergeant restlessly. "There's always someone hopping in and out, and they never seem to go to sleep."

"I think we should find Delaney," said Professor Daly suddenly. "I'm not happy about him at all."

"That poor man wouldn't hurt a fly," said the sergeant. "He's as innocent as a new-laid egg."

"I know," said Daly. "That's why I want to find him. I think our murderer may see his possibilities—oh, come along, for heaven's sake." He paused on his way to the door to add, with a kind of pleading intensity: "It's Badger who has made me uneasy about him."

Mike looked at him sharply and then stood up without a word to follow him out of the room. The sergeant came after, heavy-footed. By the time they had reached the corridor Daly had already opened the door of the suite opposite his own. They could see by the sudden droop of his shoulders that he had retained some hope of finding Delaney stooping over his desk, lifting his head with that innocent, gentlemanly, myopic expression, to invite him hospitably in.

Mike came closer and looked over Daly's shoulder into the room. It had plainly been occupied by Delaney for a very long time. Masses of papers, handwritten in faded ink, were heaped everywhere, coated with layers of dust which varied in thickness according to the length of years of the pile. Magazines and newspapers had collected in drifts in the corners. The desk was a foot deep in still more papers, scattered about with a kind of wild abandon as if a frantic mouse had been gathering nesting material among them. Daly crossed quickly to the desk and looked down at the papers. He lifted one or two of them and said sharply:

"This is odd. A newly written article torn across, and look how the creases go here. You can see that he grabbed a handful of papers quickly from the top. This is not like Delaney." He glanced around the room. "Some newspapers gone, too. See where there is a clean patch among the dust. Oh, I don't like this."

"Down to the hall," said Mike. "Lewis may have seen him."

Lewis was angry and resentful when he found three determined faces glaring at him. He wasted an agonizing minute before he admitted that he had seen Delaney go down the stairs carrying a bundle of papers, just before Mike and Daly had come in.

155

"Why did you not tell us?" Daly thundered, in a voice that made old Lewis jump in his aged skin and bite his tongue.

He wept like a baby as he answered:

"You didn't ask me. And I thought you were my friend, Professor Daly——"

"Oh, go roll your hoop!" Daly shouted, as he charged out into the quadrangle.

He was whimpering like a dog when Mike caught up with him. The sergeant followed, keeping a forceful silence. Daly looked up at the smooth brick façade with its lighted windows and groaned:

"Where to begin, that's the question! And the wind has come up."

The night had clouded over and a heavy wind was moving through the trees in the park behind them. Here, in the shelter of the quadrangle, they could only hear its intermittent roar. Then Daly put his hand on Mike's arm and pointed to the corner of the quadrangle that adjoined the President's Lodging. While they watched a deep red glow ripened and spread behind the upstairs windows. Daly plunged across the grass to the door in the corner. The sergeant pounded back to the main hall, where the telephone was, while Mike flitted after Daly as light as a shadow. A sudden gust of wind seemed to sweep them on with a derisive whistle. Daly wrenched the door open and held it until Mike was inside. Then he closed the door and they stood still to listen.

Now the glow of light came down the well of the great oak stairway that mounted from the hall. Above them they could hear a crackle like rifle-fire, with a long roar, like the sound of a blacksmith's bellows, breaking through at intervals. Smoke drifted gently downwards.

Mike was first up the stairs. Daly followed him more slowly, feeling the weight of every one of his seventy-four years. At the half-landing he paused and looked upwards. All the doors stood open up there, so that he could see the sheets of flame that filled the rooms. Mike was sitting on the top step of the stairs, beside Professor Delaney, whose face in the light of the fire bore the look of a man whose life's dream has at last come to fruition.

"You'll come with us now, Professor," Mike was saying persuasively. "Look, here comes Professor Daly to ask you to come."

"I've done it, John," said Delaney. His voice was sharp and vibrant with fulfilment. "I swore I would do it before I would retire. Now I will always be remembered at King's College." He cocked an eye towards the conflagration behind him and stood up. "That", said Professor Delaney, "will finish the rats!"

16

They got Delaney out into the quadrangle just as the first fire-engine shrieked up the avenue. A sudden enveloping blast of smoke had frightened him in the midst of his exultation, so that now he clung to Professor Daly in a way that made the older man stagger and almost lose his balance. Mike looked with compassion on the two of them, clutched in a kind of crazy waltz under the walls of their burning College. Hearing the fire-engine, people had begun to pour out into the quadrangle. Quickly Mike set Daly to the task of directing them all to the shelter of the chemistry building. Milligan, who had been working late on an experiment at the bench in his big lecture theatre, received them with guarded hospitality.

The extra policemen arrived just then and they took up positions, rather pointedly, at the various doors and windows. At the upper end of the room Delaney was telling an enraptured audience of students exactly how he had lifted up the floor-boards, ignoring the hard, glittering gaze of the watching rats, and had lit sheets of paper and pushed them underneath.

"Smoke them out," said Delaney earnestly. "That's the only way with rats."

A tall gangling student at the back of the group burst into a wild guffaw, while his big ears twitched. His friends suppressed him and gently urged Delaney to tell them more, but he had been disturbed at not being taken seriously, and he retreated into injured silence.

Meanwhile, Mike had been reassured by the firemen that they would be able to confine the fire to the set of rooms where it had started. These had been used as a natural history museum and were full of stuffed birds and animals, which had burned with the intensity of incendiary bombs. One by one they were extinguished, however, and the firemen threw the wet carcases out of the windows on to the grass. Where the fire burned fiercest a twisted, red-hot mass of metal dared anyone to come near. Mike left the men with their hoses turned on it so that it sizzled and spat, and went to hammer at the front door of the President's Lodging.

Nellie appeared at once in a long white nightdress inadequately covered by an overcoat.

"I was out to see what all the noise was for," she said breathlessly. "I thought the house would be down around us."

"It's all right," Mike said. "The men say you can stay here quite safely."

"I know," said Nellie witheringly. "I asked them. Mrs. Bradley is in the drawing-room if you want to see her."

"If you please," said Mike, and added after a moment: "I would not have let you be burned up without warning, you know."

"I wouldn't believe your Bible oath on it, sir," said Nellie over her shoulder, as she led him to the drawing-room door.

Mrs. Bradley agreed at once to let him use the house for his own purposes, and she answered his questions with surprise. Like a shipwrecked sailor she seemed too tired to be afraid. He thought it strange that she had not asked him if she might go to an hotel for the night.

Back at the chemistry building he found that the company had split into two groups. The students formed by far the larger one, of course. Bubbling over with delight they had burst into subdued song. They had a large repertoire of songs about fires, and disasters at sea, and cruel parents who slighted their anaemic daughters-in-law until they curled up and died, and young ladies who were led astray by experienced noblemen. As Mike came in at the door a short, stout student with a light tenor voice was carolling tunefully with his eyes closed:

> "Oh, happy, happy is the maid
> That's born from beauty free—
> It was my lovely rosy cheeks
> That's been the dule o' me."

159

The long sigh of his friends was like the breathing of a summer sea. Mike gave them one glance of affection before turning to the second and less carefree group.

The only one of these who seemed content was Milligan. He was boiling a blue liquid in a beaker over a gas-flame, stirring it now and then with a glass rod. The others stood around him, watching intently, as if they were a class. Sodia was there, having come to fetch her father, as she explained quickly. Hamilton looked strangely naked without his smile. Mr. Leahy stood beside Fox, looking anxious. He had been visiting Fox and had stayed late, and now it seemed he was not going to be let go home until morning, he said querulously. The nearest student of the other group caught the words and chanted:

> "*We won't go home until morning,*
> *We won't go home at all!*"

"Just you wait until to-morrow," Fox threatened through gritted teeth. "You won't get away with this."

"They laugh so that they will not weep, Foxy," said Daly gently. "Let them alone."

He glanced anxiously at Mike, who responded at once by saying:

"Mrs. Bradley says we may go over to her place. It will be much better."

"Crabbed age and youth cannot live together," said Daly. "Come along, Hamilton. And Sodia."

"Very funny," said Burren rudely. "I don't feel any need for your particular kind of variety show to-night, Daly."

Though Daly's only response to this was a raised eyebrow, still it was plain that he was displeased. Burren strutted a little as he followed the others out of the theatre. Mike took Delaney by the arm and led him out. Delaney clutched his sleeve like a nervous child. Milligan regretfully turned off the gas and came last, with a warning to the Guard on duty to see that no one touched his bench. He caught up on Daly as they walked across to the quadrangle and said:

"It would be very handy to have a Guard permanently stationed in the lab. I have never left my apparatus with a

160

greater sense of security than I did just now." He looked sharply at Daly and said: "Did your thin friend find out about you and Helen?"

"Yes," said Daly, "but I think I convinced him that there was nothing in it. It's unpleasant to have these old stories brought to light, however."

"You could have her back now," Milligan suggested gently.

"I think not," said Daly, after a moment. "I hope she doesn't expect it. If I were younger, perhaps. But I have so few years left now in which to enjoy life. Just compare her with Mary O'Leary, and you'll understand my lack of enthusiasm— Hyperion to a satyr. Oh, hang it, that's unchivalrous. Do you think my duty lies with Helen?"

"I think she hasn't done badly," said Milligan judicially. "Just don't look apologetic and everything will be all right."

Mike waited until they were all assembled on the doorstep before wringing the bell. Mrs. Bradley herself opened the door this time. She led them straight to the drawing-room, where she had put fresh wood on the fire and had ranged chairs around almost as if she liked having visitors at two o'clock in the morning. Those of her guests who had hated her late husband seemed to find it impossible not to look around the room in a possessive, patronizing way which showed clearly their satisfaction that the house would now revert to the College. Exasperated, Mike wondered how many more days of them he could have tolerated. Mr. Leahy seemed to be the only one who felt uneasy at being entertained so soon in the dead man's house.

Complaining of the cold, Delaney trotted across to the fire and stood with his hands spread out, warming himself. Then suddenly a light went on in his face as the fire reminded him of his recent exploit. He began to tell Mrs. Bradley about it, and then he paused and asked anxiously:

"Do you think I did right? Do you, really? Things were getting out of hand, and the President seemed to have no idea of his responsibilities. He was quite the worst President we've had in my time, quite the worst, without a doubt. Don't you agree?"

161

He looked at her over his spectacles, so compellingly that she had to tell him he had done well to save the College when those who should have done it had failed. She smiled at Delaney's delight in this tribute. Daly, standing by, pretended not to hear, lest she might see his gratitude and build too much on it. He went to sit at the far side of the room from her, next to Milligan. Delaney sat on the sofa as close as he could to Mrs. Bradley, whom he now regarded with adoration. Hamilton and Sodia sat together, and Fox took the big armchair at the far side of the fire. Burren sat opposite him in another. Leahy took a straight chair and placed it with its back to the wall, near the door, as if he wished to be as uncomfortable as possible.

"I want you all to tell me about the last time that you saw Bradley alive," said Mike in a conversational tone, from the hearthrug. "Try to remember if there was a forewarning of suicide in anything that he said to you."

"What about Badger and Gleeson and Donovan and all the others?" Burren asked peevishly. "Why do you pick on us?"

"I have questioned the others," said Mike soothingly, "I and Sergeant MacCarthy. You just happen to be here. Please help me."

"We all saw him at dinner," said Burren. "You were there yourself. He didn't talk of suicide then."

"You were not all at dinner," said Mike.

"I wasn't," said Delaney sadly. "I was never at dinner here. But I saw him in the afternoon to tell him that I insisted on something being done about the rats. He said we would talk about it again to-morrow. He didn't say he would be dead."

"I wasn't at dinner here either," said Fox, "but I saw him for ten minutes in the afternoon about some routine college business."

"What was it?"

"Hours of examinations—that sort of thing. It crops up every year. He seemed his usual self."

"Neither was I here," said Milligan, "but Sodia was. Bradley and I were not friends. I think I told you about the last time I saw him, Kenny."

"Yes, thank you," said Mike. "Professor Hamilton?"

"I came with Foxy in the afternoon——"

"Don't you call me Foxy!" shouted Fox in sudden rage. "It's this kind of thing that is ruining the College. The students are at it now. I heard them."

"Sorry," said Hamilton in surprise. "I've always called you Foxy. It seems to suit you, somehow. Where was I?"

"Calling on Bradley in the afternoon," said Mike.

"Ah, yes. I came to tell him that Miss Milligan and I are getting married."

Sodia gave a little uncontrollable start of surprise and turned sharply to look at Hamilton's bland face. Then very slowly she reverted to her former position and gazed motionless at her shoes. But her colour was high and her jaw was set so rigidly that it was obvious she had to keep her mind on it. Both Mike and Daly saw quite clearly that the news of her engagement had been news to her, too. Hamilton patted her amiably as he went on:

"It's in the rules somewhere that you must tell the President if you intend to get married. Probably when the rule was made the President had the power to forbid it. What would you say, Daly?"

"The rule probably dates from the old clerical universities," Daly began, but Mike cut in:

"Perhaps you wouldn't mind reading it up for Professor Hamilton and telling him about it to-morrow. Professor Hamilton, I should be obliged if you would not try to create a diversion just now. None of us are enjoying this. And you are going to like the next part even less."

They were interested now, all right. Mike was reminded of the way in which a class of schoolboys reacts to the headmaster's announcement that someone has been guilty of a crime for which there will be terrible retribution when the author is discovered—the innocent turn pale and tremble, or even burst into tears, and the criminals only look up with a kind of wondering impersonal curiosity. He went on quickly:

"I'm sorry that we must do it this way, but I see no help for it. Each of you carries a wallet or purse of some sort. I want

163

to look through them, but I must tell you first that if anyone wishes to object he may do so. I can't compel you. You are perfectly entitled to insist on having your lawyer present——"

"I'd hate to have my lawyer see the contents of my wallet," said Burren sourly. "He'd never rest until he had transferred them to his own."

Mike paused for further comments, but no one else made any. The sergeant went heavily from one to the other and received wallets in varying stages of repair from the men and handbags from Sodia and Mrs. Bradley. He carried the bundle awkwardly to a table between the windows. Mike went across and leaned over the table, with his back to the company while the sergeant returned to his place near the door.

Conversation was difficult and slow for the next fifteen minutes while Mike opened each wallet, lifted out the contents and replaced them meticulously. The owners made a point of not looking at him. Mrs. Bradley put more wood on the fire, wrecking its structure in her nervousness so that Hamilton had to come to her aid.

Now Delaney alone seemed at ease. He smiled to himself from time to time as he remembered the discomfiture of the rats. He leaned back and stretched his legs out straight before him.

"You know, Fox," he said, in the tone of a man consulting with his chief engineer," the next place to start on would be the students' rooms. That part of the building is swarming with rats. You see them everywhere you go. And the students feed them—I'm sure of that. In my day we would never have thought of such a thing."

Daly caught Hamilton's eye and shook his head. Hamilton swallowed the laughter that had been about to burst from him, and looked for a moment as if he must blow up. No one else had shown any sign of being amused, so that Daly was doubtful if they had heard at all. This was certainly the end of Delaney, he thought sadly. He wondered if he would be able to ensure that Delaney would be made Officer-in-Charge of Rats in the mental hospital to which he would certainly be committed as

164

soon as the first two competent doctors would rise from their beds in the morning. It was a blessing that Delaney's final crossing of the border between sanity and lunacy had made him so happy. When he had been sane he had not been happy at all.

Now at last Mike turned around and began solemnly to return the wallets to their owners and the handbags to Sodia and Mrs. Bradley. As one or two people began to put them away he said:

"Please open them and make sure that everything is in order."

They did so, quickly and carelessly except for Burren, who made a great show of counting his notes, of which he seemed to have a great many. Mike watched this performance with a blank countenance, and at the end of it he asked solicitiously:

"Have I given you one too many?"

Burren snorted his appreciation. Mike turned to Fox, who was just putting his wallet into the inside pocket of his coat, and said:

"There was just one thing there that I wanted to ask you about."

"In my pocket-book?"

"Yes, if you please."

Fox handed it back, looking a little surprised. Mike fumbled through the contents and then drew out a small piece of paper.

"What is this, please?"

"Can't you read?" said Fox rudely. Daly went perfectly still. "It's a ticket for a symphony concert on the fourth of November."

Mike peered closely at the ticket.

"Rather close to the front, don't you think?" he said mildly.

"Row H, on the outside," said Fox shortly. "It's where I always go. I like to be near——"

Suddenly he realized that Mike had turned away and was putting the ticket into his own pocket-book. He jerked around and saw the sergeant behind him. He heaved himself upright and charged across the hearthrug towards the door. Then,

165

like a flash, Miss Milligan lifted her elegant foot and tripped him up. Mr. Leahy opened the door and darted outside. Fox, crashed to his full length on the floor between Burren's armchair and the sofa, was set upon by the Sergeant and Murphy, and borne helpless away.

17

So they did not go home until morning after all. After the first shock of surprise, Mrs. Bradley recovered herself and went to make tea, taking Sodia with her to help.

Mike had slipped out of the room to have a talk with Fox before he was removed in the police car. As he came back again Delaney was saying eagerly:

"Did you see what they did to Fox? All those fellows taking him away—what can it all mean? I may say I don't like it in the least—not in the least."

"It's all right," said Daly. "They have to do it. He poisoned the President, you know."

"Well, what of it? I'm sure he had plenty of provocation." He paused to reflect. "And still I suppose it is going too far. You know, it was his idea to smoke the rats out from under the floor of the Natural History Museum."

"Yes, I knew that," said Daly.

"Well, that was taking a strong measure, but poisoning the President—no, I think that was going too far. Besides, how would that affect the rats?"

He looked around triumphantly at the company. Hamilton nodded in solemn agreement. Then he said confidentially to Delaney:

"Do you know, I don't believe he *cared* about them!"

Delaney relapsed into a shocked silence. Burren looked up and said:

"I wonder why Mr. Leahy was in such a hurry to get away."

"He has not gone far," said Mike, who had been listening to Delaney with a sympathetically raised eyebrow. "I have just been talking to him. He should not have stayed so long. His kind never commits murder. He is astonished that Fox should have been so foolish as to murder Bradley."

"Why did I not see all this?" said Burren. "I always found Bradley's company extraordinarily unpleasant. But I could not discover why. He seemed to try so hard to be friendly, always pawing you, slapping you on the back, clutching you by the arm."

"He must have thought one can make friends by means of mechanical devices," said Daly.

"It may have been that," said Mike, "but I think he made another mistake, too, and one that he regretted later. He patronized you all, as if you were not quite as intelligent as himself. He had been away so long that he had forgotten what university people are like."

"But he had had connections with universities in Africa," Daly pointed out.

"That is so, but he was following the pattern of most emigrants in thinking that everyone in the old country is a fool."

"We didn't know what he was at," said Hamilton. "We still don't know."

"No, but several of you said that he was up to no good. I have no doubt that you would have found him out in due course."

Just then Mrs. Bradley came in with a tea tray. Mike remembered Daly's account of another crisis in which she had sent for tea to succour the participants. She had all kinds of little cakes and buns for them, too, almost as if she had been expecting to celebrate the arrest of her husband's murderer that evening. She certainly deserved her reputation of a good housekeeper.

"Where do you get these wonderful cakes?" Daly began, holding one appreciatively aloft. "I've never——"

He stopped abruptly and became suddenly embarrassed. Mrs. Bradley, holding the teapot, waited for the end of the sentence. When it did not come she continued to pour cups of tea, smiling a little to herself in a way that made Daly feel acutely uneasy. With a calculating eye Hamilton watched Sodia hand around plates of cake. There could be no conversation except on the subject of the murder, and Mrs. Bradley's return seemed to prohibit any further discussion of this. Mike saw Burren begin to twitch and fidget as he prepared a monumentally untactful opening remark. Then Daly noticed him, too, and quickly intervened.

"Helen, would you mind if we ask Mike to clear up this whole affair for us?" he said gently. "We may not have him here so conveniently again. And you have a right to know exactly what happened. Then you can forget it all and make a fresh start."

"How thoughtful of you, John," said Mrs. Bradley, with a look of such devotion that Daly curled up like a frightened snail in his armchair. She seemed not to notice this reaction as she finished: "Please do explain, Mr. Kenny. I can't resist an appeal like that."

"Where shall I begin?" asked Mike, avoiding Daly's eye.

"Begin with Foxy, of course," said Hamilton. "What on earth was he up to?"

"He was making five-pound notes on a printing press in the Natural History Museum," said Mike. "It was to destroy the printing press that he got Professor Delaney to burn the place down. You remember, Daly, Lewis told us a little while ago that Fox was looking for you. But it was Professor Delaney he asked for. Your names are very much alike."

"And he cared nothing about the rats," said Delaney mournfully, like a Greek chorus.

"Fox has just told me that the forgery was the President's idea," said Mike. "He says that it was Bradley who procured the plates and had the press set up. He says the President led him astray, and that he would never have thought of such a thing himself.

"Fox was an amateur criminal. Bradley knew that you can't flood the local market with forged notes. It's quite a risky business. It must be indulged in with discretion. Also, he had sent for Leahy, and they had another game on, with no room in it for Fox.

"This was where the trouble started. Fox did not want to stop making the notes. When Bradley told him to dismantle the press he refused. At first Bradley tried peaceful methods of persuasion. Finally he told Fox that he was going to lead the police to the College by distributing the notes in such a way that they could be traced. Just to show Fox that he was in earnest, he gave two of the notes to Miss Milligan yesterday afternoon to pay for the repairs to the chalice. He had warned Fox that the only thing that would save him when the hunt should begin would be the disappearance of the press.

"By this time Fox had decided to murder Bradley. Bradley had never thought of this. In the circles in which he moved there is no need for murder. Everyone is in a position to black-mail everyone else, so no one feels free to begin. Bradley was not afraid of Fox. He should have been, because Fox did not know the conventions.

"It was not easy to discover the motive of the murder. There were so many people who hated Bradley that the whole situation was complicated for us, and what is usually a good pointer became instead a source of confusion." Mike's tone was impersonal enough, but he was taking great care to look into the fire. "Bradley had tormented Professor Milligan with extraordinary ferocity, considering the smallness of his griev-ance against him. The nature of the poison, too, made me think in the beginning that there was no mystery at all—that I should just go along and take Professor Milligan away. But I was disturbed from this idea by his manner. Such a highly sensitive person as he was could not have looked so uncon-cerned if he had poisoned Bradley. In fact, I thought he would probably have told me if it was he who had done it. I wondered at one time if he had told Miss Milligan, but a conversation with her disposed of that notion.

"Immediately after I had been with Professor Milligan we had dinner, and Fox was there. Was it only this evening? Fox had not been at dinner here last night, but he said something about 'that disgraceful business of the biscuit'. It was some time afterwards that it occurred to me that no one who had been there would have told Fox about it afterwards. It was a disgraceful episode," Burren snorted angrily at this censure, "and everyone was ashamed of it. It seemed to me that the only person who would have told Fox was Bradley himself, and this would mean that Fox must have visited Bradley late last night, after we had all gone home. Now Fox tells me that this is what happened."

"Wasn't that rather a long shot?" said Hamilton mildly.

"Not as long as you might think," said Mike. "We knew that someone had been with Bradley late. Nellie found used glasses and the famous concert ticket there in the morning. It was only when Professor Daly mentioned that Bradley did not like music that I guessed that the ticket belonged to the murderer. Trying it on Fox was rather a long shot, to be sure, but I had to take a chance. Bradley was not called away from us during the evening, so his visitor must have come after we had left. Of course, one of us could have come back, but Professor Burren was the only one whose movements were unaccounted for."

"I am not a well-tempered man," said Burren. "Last night I was in such a rage at the pass to which our College had come in having that man as its President that I could not contain myself. I behaved like a boor here, and when we were leaving, Bradley *handled* me again. I walked around the grounds—up and down the river-bank—through the park—everywhere—until the small hours of the morning. I'm sorry, Mrs. Bradley. I should not say these things. But he was so *unacademic*."

He brought out the word as if it were the ultimate in vituperation.

"Now I know why you are so thin," said the placid Hamilton. "You are consuming your protective fat with these internal rages. I must teach you some philosophy."

"I should be much obliged," said Burren with savage intensity.

"Now, now, nasty temper!" said Hamilton.

Burren relaxed a little and actually managed a small, lemony smile.

"The reason why I thought of Fox at all," Mike went on hurriedly, "was that I noticed inconsistencies in his behaviour. On my first evening here he had joined with the rest in telling Professor Daly about Bradley's shortcomings. Later, however, he assured everyone that Bradley had had a heart of gold under his very rough exterior. I noticed, too, that he seemed unable to bring himself to come into Bradley's bedroom, in fact he was in tears for part of the time. I thought this rather odd. Another strange thing was that Fox did not seem surprised at finding a police inspector ready and waiting on the College premises. Bradley must have told him about me, to bring home to him the danger he was in.

"Fox had told me that Bradley had shown him the anonymous letters. Bradley had, but it was to accuse Fox of having written them. Then Professor Daly made up a good suicide theory and Fox demolished it. He had become frightened at what he had done and he made several mistakes. That was one of them. Another was in showing his dismay when he heard that Leahy was proposing to leave the country. Fox's plan was to join up with Leahy in the same way as Bradley had intended to do. Of course it would not have worked. Fox was not Bradley's calibre at all."

"You said that Leahy and Bradley had some kind of a plot on," said Burren. "He looked too good to be true, but sort of innocent."

"That innocence was Leahy's stock-in-trade," said Mike. "Leahy's job was to play the part of benefactor to the College. Later, when everyone would trust him, he was going to float a company and depart with the assets. He has done this with varying degrees of success in different parts of the world. Fox has just been telling me all this. He's madly trying to put the blame on Leahy, poor chap. Leahy and Bradley were old associates in Africa and had made a lot of money there out of mines. But Bradley had lost his—no doubt we shall find out how —and at the time of his appointment here he was almost desperate. He was getting older and he was afraid that he had lost the knack of creating confidence by his appearance. This was a new sensation for him, and it worried him a great deal, as I saw when I had coffee with him on my first evening here. So he sent for Leahy in the hope of making one good coup that would keep him in comfort for the rest of his life. Leahy was to pay Bradley a large sum of money as a sort of agent's fee. Part of it would be spent on the College, but there would be something for Bradley himself, too. Bradley wanted fifty thousand pounds, but Leahy thought the same number of dollars would be plenty. They had not reached agreement about this at the time of Bradley's death. Leahy was very dissatisfied and complained to Fox. He may have suggested then to Fox that they drop Bradley and carry on together, but of course he will not admit this now because it would have been tantamount to inciting Fox to murder Bradley.

"It was Badger who spotted that there was something wrong about Leahy. Mrs. Badger's anonymous letters upset Bradley, and frightened him off the forgery game, and were the beginning of his falling out with Fox——"

"Did you say Mrs. *Badger* wrote anonymous letters to my husband?" asked Mrs. Bradley in awed tones.

"She did," said Daly. "But she meant well. I hope you won't hold it against her."

"I'm not likely to see her again," said Mrs. Bradley faintly. "I shall probably go away."

"Why did Bradley ask me to come at all?" Daly asked, after the little pause that followed. "I wish I understood that. Surely he saw that he was risking the disclosure of all his jiggery-pokery."

"It's hard to say," said Mike. "We can only speculate about that, from what we know of his character. Remember that he really was afraid of the letter-writer. And you are not as young as you used to be. He may have thought you would not see beyond the task he had given you, and that you would be flattered at being asked at all."

"He may, indeed," said Daly, remembering Bradley's patronizing manner to him on the afternoon of his arrival. "I'm going to give the rest of my lectures no matter what happens," he finished truculently.

"Of course," said Hamilton. "Already to-day I have heard several people lamenting that you would probably not finish the series now."

"I'm very pleased," said Daly. "Frustration is bad for my liver. Where did Fox get the nitro-benzene?"

173

"He made it himself, a few days ago, in Milligan's lab," said Mike. He glanced uneasily at Mrs. Bradley, but she seemed hardly to be listening. "He carried it about in his pocket waiting for an opportunity to use it. He would have tried it when he visited the President in the afternoon, but he met Professor Hamilton on the doorstep, and they came into the house together. Fox knew that Bradley would not offer him a drink while Hamilton was waiting outside in the hall. So he planned to come back after the dinner-party so that they could talk without interruption. He told Bradley that he had decided to dismantle the printing press. Bradley did not tell Fox that he had already taken steps to draw the police to the College.

"With a poison like nitro-benzene it is difficult to say to within a few hours when it was taken. But we know that its action is accelerated if it is taken with alcohol. Bradley had sherry before dinner and two wines with the meal, and whiskey afterwards. If one of his afternoon visitors had poisoned him, he would probably have collapsed before the dinner-party was over."

"You'll have to let Mr. Leahy off," said Sodia, who had made no comment until now. "You have nothing against him. I'm very glad. He's a nice little man."

"It was Bradley's misfortune that Leahy was such a nice little man that everyone took a great interest in him," said Mike. "Bradley had thought he would be allowed to make all the arrangements about the endowment without giving any details."

"We would never have allowed it in any event," said Burren. "Fellow behaved as if he owned the College."

"Professors love having a say in that sort of thing," said Daly. "He really should have known better."

"Fox tells me that while he was with the President last night he took some of the forged notes out of his pocket and burned them to prove that he was determined to finish with that game. It was then that he dropped the ticket."

"No wonder Foxy didn't like it when I said his name suited him," said Hamilton. "Now we'll have to start off to-morrow and find a new administrative staff for our College. Ah, ah!"

he said warningly, as Burren sat up and looked interested. "Not for you, Burren. You're going to take up fishing, to teach you patience. I'm going to need patience, too, because Sodia must take her degree before we can be married."

Sodia raised her eyebrows but made no objection. Mike said to Mrs. Bradley.

"I'm afraid you'll have to stay in Dublin for a while."

Suddenly they found that they must all look at her. Slowly her eyes travelled from one to another of them, while she smiled in a queer, rather ugly way. At last she said softly:

"I'm going to live alone now. That is something I have never done in all my life. I think I'm going to like it very much indeed."

Somehow there was an end of all conversation after that. Professor Daly found himself filled with such an indecent joy that he did not trust himself to speak. He shook her hands, too heartily, and then withdrew at speed as if he feared she would bite him. The others murmured an indistinguishable word or two and followed Daly into the hall. Mike came last, leading Professor Delaney gently by the arm.

Though the quadrangle was deserted now, all the outside lights were on. Lights shone from the upper windows, too, where the students had retired to discuss, no doubt, the possibility of starting another fire some time, when a diversion should seem necessary. Sodia stopped and turned to Mike.

"I wish I had not tripped Professor Fox," she said, with bitter intensity. "I wish he had got away. Why did you not just tell him that you knew what he had done, and let him go?"

Mike did not answer for a moment. The eyes of the rest were fixed on him, except for Delaney, who drooped a little now as if he were tired. Then Mike said, carefully, as if each word had been rehearsed many times:

"There was no escape for Fox. He knew that Professor Delaney would tell everyone about the splendid idea for disposing of the rats. He had kept some of the nitro-benzene for him. And he says he knew he could always make more—for instance, if your father had happened to discover that someone had used his lab without permission, or if Professor Burren had been made President instead of himself, in succession to Bradley." The sharp note went out of his voice as he continued: "I'm sorry you had to see the end of him. There was no time to be lost, you see. Once people get the habit of interfering with the laws of nature, their whole mind and character changes. Fox is a different person now from what he was three years ago."

"I never liked him," said Burren.

"I tried to like him," said Daly, "but somehow I could never manage it. People who diet to the extent that Fox did are denying the goodness of God. He was bound to pay for that sooner or later."

Hamilton chuckled with pleasure. Then he said to Mike:

"Could Professor Delaney come and stay at Milligan's tonight? Sodia and her father will look after him. There is a bed for you, too, if you like."

Mike accepted this offer with gratitude, for he had been a little perplexed as to where Delaney should spend the remainder of the night. Hamilton's kindness and forethought were deeply consoling to him now, when he had suddenly found himself overwhelmed with weariness. Perhaps this was why he went off with the others with no more than a word to Professor Daly.

The old man stood in the quadrangle, sharply lonely, watching the little group move down the avenue. The night wind was cold. Presently he shivered, and then turned with a quick movement to go in. The hallway was deserted, and again he felt a sharp emptiness about the heart, which would have been relieved even by the aggravating presence of Lewis.

"But it's too late at night for philosophizing," he said to himself. "Everything will look different in the morning."